J. B

BORN OR BRED

(PIGS AND *MONSTERS*)

Born or Bred
(Pigs and Monsters)

J. Boote

Contents

<u>Chapter 1</u>

"It all started with a pig. Two pigs. Both literally and metaphorically. One was a big, fat bastard; the other a big, fat monster. I'll let you decide which is which."

Chapter 2

"Claire, I'd like you to tell me about the birds. About that day and why, if you can, you did what you did."

"The birds? There were lots of incidents with birds. Which one are you referring to?"

"I think you know the incident I'm talking about. The first one. That was maybe the beginning of everything that happened from then on."

"Oh, that. Okay."

Claire shows not the slightest sign of discomfort or unease as she takes a deep breath and a sip of water. And considering what she did, this tells me more than the story itself. Not a hint of remorse in her eyes or sadness for what transpired that day. This is to be expected, of course, given everything that occurred later, but I think the truly sad thing about that day was the level of violence shown to the birds, totally out of character with Claire at that time. One could argue that her later victims were not entirely free from blame, despite what she did to them, and in her eyes, at least, but this first episode of extreme violence is a real indicator of where she was heading. If only someone had known about what she did, the turmoil she was going through, had seen her doing that to the birds, we might not be here now. But, of course, given the people in her life, I don't suppose it would have made much difference.

"So, after what happened with the chickens, I guess I was really confused. I didn't understand anything that was happening to me. I guess I thought it was all perfectly normal behaviour. That everyone else went through the same thing. It never even occurred to me to ask anyone if it was normal, because it would have sounded stupid. And I didn't want to be seen as stupid. Not with everything else going on and the things being said and done.

"But anyway, after what my dad and his friends did to the chickens, I was curious. I wanted to know if the same thing happened to all other birds, so one day I just got up and went looking. It never occurred to me I was doing anything wrong or bad, because I was taught it was perfectly normal. I saw things like this on a daily basis. If I had seen what happened later with the pig, I might have done it to one of our cats or dogs instead. Probably would have actually."

She shrugs. Again, not a tear in her eyes, no indication of remorse, her speech patterns bland. Claire might as well be talking about the weather.

"So, behind the lake was a field with trees dotted about. I went searching for any birds' nests among the bushes, where I could reach them. There were quite a lot of people fishing on the lake that day because it was warm and sunny, and something told me I really didn't want them to see me doing what I wanted to do. Why, I didn't know, because as I said, to me what I was doing was normal. Like fuck, everyone probably did it. I'd seen my dad and his friends do it, having a great time. Not that anything my dad did was normal, of course, the drunken piece of shit, but...it's hard to explain. Some things felt normal because it was, like, my parents that did it to me. And our parents are supposed to love us, right? So, I kept telling myself I deserved the punishments they dished out, being starved and so on when I was young. And...and the other things he did at nights.

They were trying to teach me a lesson.

"So, while on the one hand I thought it was acceptable, normal behaviour, on the other it seemed all wrong somehow. Because I never completely understood what it was I had done wrong in the first place. I was terrified of being whipped or beaten by my parents or being locked in the shed all night without food or water, so none of it made any sense. Even what my dad did to me when he thought my mother wasn't looking, or even the things she used to say to me in front of her 'men-friends' as she called them.

"Anyway, creeping through the brambles and bushes, I finally found a bird nest with birds in it. Tiny little things, but big enough they were almost fully formed, nearly ready to fly away. I have no idea what species, and it didn't matter anyway. Not as if I was fussy. There were four of them in there. From nearby, I could hear this racket going on, probably the mother or something flying around and screeching. I think it was a blackbird. Kept flying overhead and around in circles with that constant yep-yap-yap, like a dog signalling danger. I ignored it, obviously.

"So, I picked up one bird in my hand. I remember it shat on my palm, as though it was terrified, and I thought that was funny. This stupid bird is fucking terrified of me. I thought it was pathetic even though I did the exact same thing on occasions when my dad came into my room or was drunk or angry. Or my mother, for that matter, the bitch, but I didn't see it that way then. I recalled what my dad did, but I didn't have a knife or anything so I did the next best thing. I pulled its head off.

8

"I had to twist it quite a bit. Like 360 degrees, and I heard its little neck snap, and it stopped squawking and flapping, but I carried on anyway. I twisted and pulled until its head came right off. I threw the head away then put the bird on the ground, but of course it was already dead, so it just keeled over with its feet sticking up. So I tried another.

"This time, though, I tried to do it faster. I gripped its body tight with one hand, then its head with the other and pulled as hard and as fast as I could, in my stupid mind thinking 'Well, if I don't twist its head so its neck snaps, it might work.' I couldn't do it, though. Even though it was a fragile, little thing, its fucking head wouldn't come off, so I got annoyed and just twisted it until it did. Just in case, I put it on the ground, but same thing. I realised I needed something sharp."

"So, just to clarify; you lived on a farm with various animals and poultry, and it had been the first time you saw your father do that to a chicken? You'd never heard the rather common phrase related to such things?"

"Probably, I can't remember, but it didn't matter anyway. For one thing, they seemed to be having so much fun as they killed the chicken and watched it, and I was just curious if it happened to all birds. I have to admit, it wasn't fun at all. I didn't feel anything for the stupid blackbirds. Just curiosity.

"So, I went looking for something sharp or heavy so I could just bludgeon its head so it came off. Eventually, I did. Found half a brick, so went back to the nest, picked up the third bird, and held it to the ground. Then, with the sharp edge of the brick, I smashed it into the bird's neck. It came straight off. I

9

remember I was smiling, happy I'd been clever enough to come up with a way. Its head came off, and when I put it upright on its feet, it just keeled over again, dead. I was so annoyed it hadn't started running around like the chicken, I picked up the last bird and crushed it between my palms. Not before pulling its wings off first, though. I put that fucking bird between my hands and just squeezed and squeezed, to the point the thing fucking exploded, covering me in blood and guts and feathers. My dad had cut that chicken's head off and they had all laughed as it carried on running around in circles and flapping. I guess I learned that day that it only happens to chickens."

Claire shrugs, takes another sip of water. She brings out her pack of cigarettes, spots the no smoking sign on my office door, and puts them back in her pocket.

"So how old were you when this happened, Claire?"

"Oh, about seven, almost eight, I guess. That was the first time I ever killed something. Wasn't the last though, right!"

Claire laughs for the first time today.

Chapter 3

Claire Peterson thanked the school bus driver and jumped off. It sped away to deliver the other kids to their homes spread out over the sparsely populated area. Her nearest neighbour was a five-minute walk up the road. And for a seven-year-old, it was as close as one could get to living in utter desolation yet still have neighbours. When she stepped off the bus each afternoon, she still had the ringing of the school bell in her ears, the other kids laughing and yelling, cars blaring music and horns as they sped past. Now the only thing she could hear was the howling of the wind as it blew through trees, rustling leaves and bushes or whistling across open fields. She could hear birds singing or calling, which to another might have been a pleasant experience, a break from the hustle and bustle of suburban life, but to Claire, she often wished she could swap it for that of human activity. She wouldn't feel as lonely and abandoned.

From farther down the country lane came the sound of chickens, squabbling over food perhaps, a pig grunting and snorting, ducks quacking. These were her closest neighbours because they all lived in the same field as she did. As a toddler, she had found it exciting to be among such a diverse array of animals, even being allowed to handle some of them, except the pigs, which scared her due to their size. Plus, they smelled horrible. But now, as far as she was concerned, they were as exciting as watching trees. And when she discovered for the first time that occasionally the food on her plate came directly from the creatures she used to play with and had given names to, it horrified her, and she tried to keep as big a distance as possible from them. There was also the added horror of the other kids at school taunting her for how and where she lived.

And when Claire came home from school, things weren't any easier for her. In fact, despite the cruel taunts of the kids, it was nothing compared to what she suffered here. Sometimes, even though the animals smelled foul and were dirty, she often considered spending the afternoons with them. It had to be better than what went on behind the walls of the large house behind the popular fishing lake.

She entered the winding, dirt road that led to the lake, bramble bushes on either side, the dust from the dirt track being blown up by the wind and getting on her clothes and in her face. Even for seven she was a tiny, frail figure, shorter and thinner than most other kids her age. Occasionally, teachers would ask her if she was eating okay at home. She lied and said yes, but the way the teachers looked at her suggested her bright, blue eyes were giving away the truth. Her maths teacher, Mrs Hemsby, would often stroke Claire's shoulder-length, black hair, sometimes helping her to untie the knots that inevitably formed in it from being unbrushed so often. Mrs Hemsby occasionally asked her if her mother was washing it for her on a regular basis and if so, what shampoo she was using. Claire lied about that, too, saying she showered every night but couldn't remember the name of the shampoo. It was only technically a lie, because Claire couldn't recall the last time she had used proper shampoo. Normally, her mother made her use washing-up liquid—it was cheaper, and if it was good enough to wash dishes, it was good enough to wash hair.

Other kids would smirk at her regarding the clothes she wore, often the same trousers and blouses worn over several days because her mother hadn't bothered washing the rest. Inevitably, they were often covered in grime and dust from the farm and walking down this long, dirty track. Her black trainers—black so they wouldn't show the grime and smudges—bore holes in them, but her parents ignored her pleas for new ones. Sometimes, when she didn't have sports, she would go to school with no underwear on because they stuck to her from being worn for so many days in succession. But wearing no underwear meant the insides of her thighs chaffed from constant rubbing. A lesser evil.

The dirt track opened onto the field where Green Lake was situated. Several cars were parked around the perimeter. Claire had no idea about fishing, but it seemed to be popular with the fishermen, always people dotted around the large lake, sat there huddling around a blanket or sprawled on the grass soaking up the sun. It was just as well it was popular, because Claire knew one of their main sources of income came from charging them for the right to fish there. That was her mother's job, to wander around the lake two or three times a day to collect whatever she charged. If anyone left before she took their money, Claire would hear her mother yelling and shouting for hours afterwards, hurling insults at the air while simultaneously grabbing the foul-smelling bottle of alcohol she drank. Claire tried to hide during those moments.

On the other side of the field, to her right, was where the animals and poultry were kept. That was her father's job, usually, to feed and clean out their pens, collect the eggs the chickens, ducks, and geese left behind, and occasionally slaughter one or several for food. Recently she had been given the task of feeding them and collecting the eggs when she came home from school or first thing in the mornings at the weekend because more often than not her father was drunk or asleep somewhere. Her dad said she was old enough to help now that she was seven.

She couldn't see the huge bulk of her father anywhere or hear him laughing loudly with friends, normally with beers in their hands, so she assumed her parents were in the house. With any luck, both would be taking a nap. If that was the case, she might be able to make a sandwich without being seen and thus scolded and slapped for eating too much. And Claire was very hungry, as almost always.

She opened the front door as quietly as possible, barely breathing and tense, half-expecting to hear yelling and fighting as was so often the case. This had been going on since Claire could remember, but she never got used to it. It made her bladder loose every time, and when her parents, usually her mother, started throwing things about and saying disgusting things Claire barely understood properly, all she wanted to do was run from the house and never come back. She often fantasised about doing just that, especially when she had the nightmares at night, although for some reason they didn't feel like nightmares. They were too real—her dad standing over her as she slept, and the next day she would wake up with slight bruising on her thighs. He told her she must have rubbed her legs together during a particularly vivid dream.

Fortunately, it was quiet inside the house. The occasional thud came from upstairs, which meant her mother was either prancing about her bedroom, as she often did, or getting ready to take a nap. Either way, she had no intention of disturbing her. Claire took off her coat, hung it up on the hanger, and took off her trainers. If she forgot to do so and traipsed dirt and mud around the house, it would mean going without supper or being slapped across the face. Or both. Then she would be made to scrub the floors everywhere until Mum was satisfied.

She tiptoed across the worn, brown carpet and peeked in the living room. She heard her father's snoring before she saw him. It reminded her of the pigs grunting down in their pens. Sometimes, even though she loved her father, she couldn't help thinking he looked like one sometimes with his massive stomach hanging over the top of his filthy jeans, sweaty red face, and short, close-cropped, blonde hair. He grunted again, scratched absently at his nose, and resumed sleeping. Claire left him to it and went to the kitchen. The fridge was almost permanently empty, but she found some cheese slices that wouldn't be noticed missing if she only took a couple and made herself a sandwich. She was ravenous, because on the occasions her mother remembered to make her a packed lunch for school, it was invariably devoid of anything that would take away a perpetual hunger. Once she'd finished, she had a glass of water—nothing else to drink except alcohol—and headed upstairs.

She knew she shouldn't do it and would never be able to explain why she did. Morbid curiosity perhaps, or maybe it was the alien sound of her

15

mother giggling then grunting and swearing. Until now, she would never dare interrupt her mother or go into her bedroom without permission or having been directly called in, but she couldn't understand what was going on in there. A man's voice could be heard, too, and he was saying horrible things to her, calling her names and saying he was going to do things to her Claire didn't understand. But instead of sounding afraid, Claire's mother would laugh. Then there would come a loud slap and grunting and panting. It was obviously happening on the bed, too, because it was rocking violently back and forth, the head rest banging against the wall.

Her brain was telling her to ignore it and go to her room, but it also sounded like someone was hurting her mother. Maybe she should go tell her dad, she wondered, but if it was mum just messing about, he would be extremely annoyed at being woken for nothing. And the last thing she wanted was to annoy her dad. She still had bruises on her arm from the last time. Instead, Claire opened the door and peered in.

What she witnessed made absolutely no sense at all. Her first thought had been to rush to her mother's aid and beat off the horrible, naked man that was hurting her. But if this was the case, why was she grinning? She shouldn't be, she should be begging to be left alone, for him to get off her. She was semi-naked, too, wearing only stockings and suspenders and high heels, but there were also straps and ropes wrapped tightly around her breasts and neck, so tight the flesh around them was bloated and red raw.

She couldn't avoid noticing his thick, erect penis, an alien thing, the first time she had ever seen one except her father's when he used to parade around the house naked in summer or leaving the shower and casually strolling to his bedroom to get dressed. In her dreams she thought she might have seen it too. But this was totally different. She had been so used to seeing her parents naked she thought it was normal, but something suggested to her this was far from normal. He was holding what looked like a thin stick, too, beating his mother across the breasts with the straps at the tip of the stick.

It took them a few seconds to realise Claire was standing at the entrance, frozen, unsure what to do or say. Then they both turned and saw her, the man mid-stroke.

Her second thought was that she was in a world of trouble for entering without permission. Her mother was going to lock her in the shed again all night or worse. Beat her with a stick, make her go to school in filthy, unwashed clothes so the other kids could see what a dirty, little pig she was. Stub out her cigarette on her chest or back, which made her scream for hours. She opened her mouth to apologise, plead with her not to punish her, but a strange thing happened. Something she would never have expected.

The man looked shocked, glancing from Claire to her mother and back again, slowly backing away, trying to hide his erect penis from her, but her mother, instead of screaming at her to get the hell out, laughed.

"Hit me again," she demanded to the man.

He looked even more surprised but immediately did as he was told, as though her slave.

There came a loud slap as the end of the whip left a red mark across her chest. Claire flinched, tears in her eyes, not understanding why her mother was telling the man to hit her. It had to hurt really bad. But her mother had a funny look in her eyes, sparkling as though she was enjoying it a lot.

"Don't just stand there, Claire, come on in!"

But Claire couldn't move. She was frozen in place, wanting to turn and run from this hideous scene but unable to will herself to move.

"Aww, what's wrong?" slurred her mother. "Don't ya wanna come and play? Try it! You might even like it. Look how big his dick is. We could share it. There's plenty for everyone."

She burst into a hysterical fit of giggles, gripped the man's penis tight, and began to drag him closer to her.

"You kids are all fuckin' the minute you're born these days. Might as well start now, kid. C'mon! Come and suck it with me."

Claire turned and bolted from the room to her own bedroom. She jumped in bed fully clothed and covered herself with the blanket, as if this might hide the terrible scene from her mind.

It was this scene where Claire had her first association of pain with joy. It wouldn't be her last.

***

"I never wanted a dummy, you know. For as long as I remember, no matter how much I cried as a toddler, whenever my mother tried to put a dummy in my mouth I would cry and spit it out. My mother never understood and would get angry because she didn't know what else to do. But I hated it yet at the same time never really knew why, either. It brought back bad memories."

"And how early on in your life do you recall this happening? Rejecting the dummy?"

"Since I remember. I used to have nightmares—or what I thought were nightmares—where I'd be choking and couldn't breathe. I'd wake up panting and crying in fear, thinking I was dying. I think now it was going on since I was born. As a baby. I watched something on YouTube about how some going through a traumatic experience can recall events that happened to them as babies, and I definitely recall wearing a nappy at the time when these so-called nightmares occurred."

"And what was happening, Claire? Can you talk about it?"

"Oh, for sure. Now he's dead it doesn't matter. The first time I really remember it happening, my dad came into my room one night. I don't know how long he was laying there, completely naked, but I woke up and saw him. It scared the crap outta me, thinking it was a monster or something. But he smiled and hushed me, brushing my hair away from my face. Even then I got the sense something wasn't right. I couldn't understand why he was in my bed naked, and his filthy cock wasn't as I'd seen it before. It was rigid, fucker had the biggest hard-on of his life. It was throbbing. He was breathing heavily and obviously excited. Then he leaned over and kissed me on the lips. His breath was disgusting, smelling of booze and tobacco.

"I asked him what was wrong. In my naivety, I asked him if he'd had a nightmare, too, like me, and wanted the company, and he smiled and said yes, he was scared and wanted to cuddle up to me, so I let him. Then he asks me to hold him tighter, and I could smell his sweat. Even then he smelled like the pigs, but as I've got my arms wrapped around his chest, he takes my hand and wraps it around his cock and sighs.

"I almost jumped, knowing even then I shouldn't really be touching it, but he whispers in my ear it's all okay, I'm just showing Daddy how much I love him. His hand covering mine, he starts bringing my hand up and down, jerking him off. I didn't like it but was too scared to say anything. Whenever I upset him, especially when he was drunk, he could get vicious and nasty, twisting my nipples or the cheeks of my arse, fingernails digging in."

"Can you recall how old you were during this particular incident?"

"I think I was four because just before starting school the first time, my mother cut my hair real short. I guess she was worried even then about Child Services being informed something was wrong. But I know for sure it was already going on. I recognised the taste. So, after a few seconds of this he pushes himself up and says that if I really loved him, like all good girls love their parents, I would kiss it. But using my tongue as well. I didn't want to, but really, what choice did I have? So, I go to kiss it, using my tongue as he said, and then he pushed it into my mouth. I gagged, so he pulled it out a bit then pushed it back in again. In, out, in, out.

"At the time, I didn't quite understand why, but he was sobbing. I thought it was because he was so happy I was showing him how much I loved him, but now we know different. It was the shame and he couldn't stop himself. Long story short, he kept doing it until he came. I tried to spit it out, but there was so much I ended up swallowing most. That's how I know it happened before—the taste. And this is why I refused and cried every time my mother tried to shove a dummy in my mouth."

The way Claire tells this horrible story is completely without emotion, as though chatting with friends about her weekend. I had tears in my eyes just listening to her. And given what happened to her father later, on this occasion I'm inclined to say he deserved everything she did. I keep asking myself if the mother knew and her thoughts about it, although tragically, I think I already know.

"That's horrific, Claire. How long did this go on for?"

"For years. Several times a week. He must have been getting confident that I hadn't told anyone, because he started fucking me too. Like, not enough to break the hymen so my mother would find out, but he'd push it in just enough for me to feel it. Then, when he was close to coming he'd put it in my mouth or make me give him a hand job, always careful not to stain the sheets. Which were filthy anyway, so no one would have noticed. He did this until I got arrested and taken away. I bet that scared the fuck outta him, thinking I was gonna tell the police everything, but I didn't."

I have no words.

"Actually, that's something of a lie. About not breaking my hymen, I mean."

"What are you talking about, Claire?"

"Reflecting on it later, I figured I must have imagined it all until I did a little research because it seems impossible. A girl's body that young, it should be physically impossible to do such things, but apparently not. There's a girl from Peru who once had a caesarean at just five-years-old. Can you believe that?"

This is true, but I have a feeling what I'm about to hear is going to make everything else seem trivial by comparison.

"I heard about the case, but please, carry on."

"Anyway, I think I was around seven, had just turned. Not long before I killed Tania, a year maybe. I remember waking up one morning and there was blood on the bed sheets and my vagina was throbbing badly. It was so painful. I don't know how I even slept that night. I guess shock or something, dunno. I remember checking down below and saw there was blood splatter on the insides of my thighs. I didn't know about periods or anything then, of course, and all I could think was that I'd somehow hurt myself and was going to bleed to death.

"I started sobbing. Panicking. I was just about to run downstairs to my mother and tell her what was going on when my dad walked in the room. He hugged me and stroked my hair, saying everything was going to be okay. That perhaps I'd walked into something during the night, on the way to the toilet maybe, and that I shouldn't bother Mum about it. She was in a bad mood, he said, and didn't want to be disturbed. So he took me to the bathroom, cleaned me up, and changed the bedsheets, then told me to get ready for school. I could barely walk, so he drove me into school saying he had to pick up grain and stuff for the pigs. I think I was in some kind of trance all day, because I don't remember a thing. Except when I went to the toilet, and when I looked in the bowl afterwards it was a pinkish-yellow colour. I dare not go to the toilet for the rest of the day.

"He came and picked me up from school afterwards, too, asked me how I was and not to forget that it was our secret. He brought chocolate bars and stuff with him to bribe me into keeping quiet, obviously. But he never thought any more would come of it; of course he didn't. It was about six weeks later when the morning sickness started."

I cannot believe I'm hearing this. I know what she did to her father later, and to an extent, I always thought it was a heinous and terrible thing she did. Now, I think I would have done the same thing…

"Now, my mother, as you've probably guessed by now, was a tight bitch. She would get fucking batshit crazy if anything was wasted. Every single penny had to be accounted for. Food was never thrown out. At the very most, it would be used to feed the pigs. If I refused to eat whatever shit she made, like broccoli or certain vegetables, she would grip my cheeks between her fingers, force my mouth open, and shove it down my throat. No one was allowed to leave the table until every morsel was eaten. If something got accidently broken she would go into a mad rage. If I took too long in the shower or left a lightbulb on, she would grab whatever was laying about and smack me hard on the back or buttocks, leaving these terrible, red whelps.

"So, when the morning sickness started, just the sight of food sometimes made me feel sick. But because she forced me to eat it, I had no choice but to do so. And obviously, there were mornings I vomited it all back up again. Well, she went fucking mad. I remember she grabbed the back of my head and rammed my face into that pool of vomit and made me eat it all up, literally licking the remains off the table with my tongue until it was all gone. All lumpy and gooey and sticky. Then, she'd kick me out to go to school and I'd vomit once more on the grounds. That happened a few times."

I feel sick just hearing this. Dear God…

"So you have to understand what came later. When I say my mother was a penny pincher, nothing went to waste. When money was tight, she'd reuse the same teabag over and over. Showers—when I was allowed to have one—were limited to three minutes max. The washing machine was only used when literally not a single extra sock would fit in the machine, and most of the time I wore dirty clothes anyway. But it was with food that she was so obsessed. She'd go to all different supermarkets to buy stuff, instead of just one. Like if milk was two pennies cheaper down the road, she'd go there to buy it, and so on. A dead rabbit or duck or whatever was found on the farm? Instead of throwing it away, she'd cook it, regardless of how it died. If she accidently dropped an egg, for example, she would scream and hurl insults at everything and everyone.

"I'm telling you this so you understand. She was obsessed with saving money to the point of it being a serious fucking problem.

"My dad kept it secret about fucking me and hiding the bedsheets, but never did he ever think I would get pregnant as a result. Well, I did, didn't I. At nights, he'd come into my room asking how I was and I would tell him I felt sick all the time and my tummy and down below really ached, and then I think he knew. You could see the blood drain from his face as the realisation hit him.

"He went to a pharmacy and bought one of those pregnancy kits. He bought two more as well, just to confirm. But yep, I was pregnant, and within a short time it was starting to be noticeable. There was no way I should be getting fatter considering my mother was literally starving me. And obviously she noticed. She couldn't believe it. Refused to, in fact, like me, thinking it was physically impossible. I don't remember her ever asking who the father was, but I think she knew anyway. Probably had plenty of discussions with my father about that one when I was asleep. But I did often hear them arguing about what was gonna happen. That I'd be put in care, they'd both go to prison, they'd lose the farm, everything. So, no one was to know and something had to be done about it.

"I remember one day when I was about three months pregnant, she punched me in the stomach for no reason. Now I know why, of course, but it didn't work. Then, despite it being summer, she made me wear baggy shirts and jumpers to hide the bulge, and I knew even then she was getting extremely worried about what was going to happen. There was no way they could take me to a doctor or clinic for an abortion, and they certainly weren't going to let me keep it, so they did the next best thing.

"My father had a friend, a retired doctor. I later learned that he agreed to do it in exchange for one of the pigs as payment. He came over one afternoon. They took me upstairs and laid me down in the spare bedroom. I was terrified, screaming, begging my parents to not let him do whatever he was going to do, because even then, see, I truly thought I was going to have a baby and I'd have someone to play with. I fantasised about playing with my baby as though it was a new doll I'd just been gifted. I knew about babies and how they came about because I'd heard older kids at school talking about them.

"The doctor injected me with something. I felt a little pressure on my stomach and a horrible pain in my vagina, and then a few minutes later he was holding up this tiny little thing with the instrument in his hand. It looked only slightly smaller than those birds I killed, barely human. He handed it to my mother, who looked at it as though it was something foul and disgusting that the cat just brought in. We ate it that night."

"Wait, no. Stop there. You're lying, Claire. There is no way you can expect me to believe what yo—"

"I told you, she wasted nothing. She made a stew with it that night, and we all ate it, and together the three of us promised we would never say another word about it. I ate my own baby. My father ate his own son or daughter, and he slurped up that stew like it was the best thing he'd ever eaten. Didn't even know if it was a boy or girl. I cried for days afterwards, and every time I did, my mother would slap me across the face and tell me to shut up. If I didn't, she'd lock me in the shed overnight until I promised not to cry again. So there you have it. And you wonder why I turned out like I did. Oh, and the very next night my dad was back in my room again, but he never tried to fuck me again. Of course he didn't."

Chapter 4

Claire didn't want to do it but couldn't think of any more excuses. She'd tried them all, but now her brain refused to come up with anything new. It was dirty and filthy. It was smelly. They would get into trouble if she got dirty, which was practically guaranteed. Her parents were asleep or busy. She had lots of homework. But the new girl, Gayle, kept insisting, and Claire didn't know what to say anymore. In a way, she did want to show Gayle the farm and the lake and the house, but at the same time, even though Gayle seemed nice and was the only one that spoke to her without making fun of her, she might do just that after seeing the conditions in which Claire lived.

No one had been to Claire's home before. She didn't have any friends anyway, because most of the kids at school said she was smelly and poor, and they avoided her as though this condition might be contagious. But since Gayle had started chatting with Claire a few weeks ago, she thought they might have become friends. Gayle wore long, blonde hair mostly tied back in a ponytail; she had large, brown, almond-shaped eyes. Her clothes were always spotlessly clean, fresh clothes worn each day, and her trainers were fabricated by Nike. Claire would love to have owned a pair of Nikes, but her parents said they were too expensive, so she had to make do with the cheap ones from the Chinese-owned shop in town. Gayle was confident and had a bubbly voice and a laugh that made everyone else smile. All the other kids liked Gayle, so when she had started chatting to Claire one afternoon at playtime, Claire had been instantly on edge, assuming Gayle's friends were hiding somewhere, chuckling, as Gayle pretended to be nice to her. It had been several days of Claire expecting at any moment for Gayle to say something horrible and derogatory to her then run off howling with laughter, but it never happened.

And now, after Claire told her that she lived on a farm-like place with a big lake and pigs and ducks and chickens and everything else, Gayle's eyes had lit up and she wanted to come visit. Initially, Claire had been horrified. There was no way she could take Gayle home. Her dad might be embarrassing, as he always was when he drunk that nasty-smelling stuff, slurring and stumbling about. Or her mother. What if they arrived at the farmhouse and her mother was acting weird again with that man or another like the other day? Nothing more had been said about it, as though her mother had completely forgotten, but Claire had had nightmares for days afterwards, imagining that man coming into her room at night and whipping her with that stick then making her do things to him as her mother had made him do. It hadn't been the first time Claire had seen strange men coming in and out of the house, either, usually when dad was asleep or in town. Claire would die of shame if that happened, and now that she finally seemed to have a genuine friend, Gayle would run screaming and tell everyone at school, and that would mean Claire being lonely and humiliated again. It couldn't happen.

But it did.

Gayle refused to take no for an answer. "Please, Claire! I wanna see the pigs and the other animals.

I've never seen pigs before up close. They're cute. I asked my mum and she said it was okay. That when I'm ready, to phone and she'll come pick me up. Please!"

"But, the bus drops us off at the bottom of a dirty road and it's smelly and full of dust. You'll get dirty. And the pigs stink!"

"I don't care. I wanna see 'em. I won't be your friend anymore if you don't."

Claire didn't really believe that part, and she did want to show Gayle around the grounds, but that nagging doubt about her parents' behaviour worried her. Unless, of course, they never went in the house. They could see the animals and the lake, and by that time Gayle would be hungry and tired and would want to go home.

"Okay, but we can't go in the house, only outside."

"Yay!"

Two days later, they arranged to meet after school and take the bus together. Gayle had her mother's phone number written down on a piece of paper and carefully guarded in her school bag. Gayle told Claire that Gayle's mother would probably be phoning to check on them anyway, which made Claire even more nervous. Her mother didn't like answering the phone, especially if it wasn't anything important. Claire told her mother that Gayle would be coming over to see the animals and lake, and the woman barely shrugged her shoulders and ignored her, lighting a cigarette, blowing the horrible smoke in her face, and walking off.

"Don't expect me to feed 'er as well, you know. You cost enough to feed as it is."

Given that Claire was almost always hungry, she didn't understand this comment. Food must be really expensive to buy, she reasoned.

It was a warm, sunny day for mid-April so neither Claire nor Gayle wore jackets. As always, Claire wore dark trousers so the stains and grime wouldn't be as visible, while Gayle wore a yellow dress. Claire was jealous. She didn't own a single dress, only dark trousers and jeans, which according to her mother lasted longer.

She was nervous as they rode the bus together, other boys making jokes about Claire and making grunting pig noises. Both pretended to ignore the kids, chatting together about random subjects. It was only when Gayle learned that Claire had no TV in her room, no games consoles, nothing except a few books and board games, she was silent for a while as though offering a mark of respect.

The bus stopped and they climbed down. Claire was always a little scared when she got off the bus, here in what to her was the middle of nowhere. She could fall and hurt herself and no one would know. She'd often begged her mother or father to come and meet her, but they said they were too busy and she was old enough by now to come home on her own. It had been six months since they stopped coming to collect her, and the bus driver always waited until she was down the dirt track and out of view before he sped off.

"Wow, I've never been out here before. It's really quiet," said Gayle.

"In winter, I get scared 'cause it's dark. I think I hear and see things."

"Doesn't your parents come and meet you?"

She shook her head. Claire started walking. She didn't want to talk about her parents anymore. As they headed down the dirt track, she changed the subject, telling Gayle about some of the funny things the animals did and the funny noises they made. They reached the opening onto the car park and the lake to their left, the animals to their right.

"Wow, this is huge! Do you own all this?"

"Yes. My grandparents used to live here, then they died a few years ago and it got left to us. I used to like it, but I don't anymore. I want to live closer to you and the playgrounds and parks. It's boring here. And smelly."

To that, Gayle laughed. "It is a bit smelly. It must be the pigs. My dad told me last night, after I said I was coming here, that pigs lie and roll around in their own poop. Is that true?"

"Yep! I've seen them do it."

"That's gross! I'm never eating bacon again."

"That's what I said! But I love bacon when mum or dad make it, so I still eat it."

Claire pointed to where the animals were, although it wasn't necessary; they could hear them perfectly well. Gayle practically ran to where the various pens were. Claire ran after her, laughing for the first time she could remember on these grounds. She'd forgotten what it was to laugh around here.

There were seven pigs, each in separate pens; six sows, and a boar to use for breeding purposes. The boar was a Spanish Jabalí, huge and dark with tusks that reminded Claire of the sabre-toothed tigers she'd seen in nature books. Its eyes were permanently bloodshot, the animal aggressive and dangerous, and she was strictly forbidden from entering.

According to her father, the babies would be sold at the market. Other times some were kept, and when big enough these would be slaughtered. Claire had never seen this happen but had heard her father talk about it, and it had shocked her. It was then she stopped giving them names and pretending they were her friends.

Gayle kept her distance but seemed fascinated by the huge creatures as they grunted at her from behind their brick walls. Then the smell must have hit her because she backed away even farther and suggested they go look at the ducks and geese instead, kept on their own small pond away from the fishermen. Their wings had been clipped so they couldn't fly away. Claire knew that sometimes these made their way to the dinner table too.

As Gayle squatted and tried to stroke the ducks swimming happily around the pond, Claire's stomach suddenly lurched. And it wasn't from the smell of the birds either. Her father was heading their way, walking unsteadily, a big silly grin on his face, a can of beer in his hand.

"Oh no," she muttered.

Her father saw the two girls and his grin widened.

"Hey, let's go," said Claire.

Gayle looked up surprised and saw the huge man approaching them. She looked a little concerned herself, and Claire wasn't surprised—he was an intimidating man with his large bulk and well over six feet tall.

"Well, what have we got here?" he slurred. "And who are you?" he asked, glaring straight at Gayle.

"Hi, Mr Peterson. I'm Gayle. Claire's my friend."

"Is that so? You didn't tell me you had a new

friend, Claire. That's very rude of you."

"Sorry."

"It's okay, I'm only jokin'. You're very cute, Gayle. You live around 'ere?"

"No. My mum will come pick me up when I'm ready to go home. I live in Belton."

"Really. Well, you come over any time you like, ain't that right, Claire?"

"Yes."

Please go away, she prayed to herself. She wasn't entirely sure why, but he made her nervous and uncomfortable, and now that she had finally made a real friend, she didn't want to scare her off. She took Gayle's hand and made to walk away.

"Hey, where ya goin' so fast? Stay and chat. I wanna hear about yer new friend. How old are ya, Gayle?"

"Seven, nearly eight."

"That's a good age. You have a boyfriend yet?"

"Eww, no. Boys are gross!"

"Hehe. You say that now. Couple of years' time you'll be beggin' for it, like all girls and women. Ain't that right, Claire? Just like yer mother. Always wanting a bit."

And then he did something that made Claire want to burst out crying in shame and embarrassment. He slapped her behind. Hard. But he didn't remove his hand straight away, either, instead rubbing his palm over her behind for a few seconds. Gayle didn't seem to understand the connotations of what he was saying, not answering him and looking at Claire confused. Fortunately, Claire's father backed away and carried on walking towards the pig pens.

Claire took a deep breath and tried to change the

subject. It was this incident that she would later associate with men as being perverts.

***

"It's so sad that you finally made a friend, a real one, yet rather than being happy and excited, it made you nervous. In case it was a trick, or as finally happened, she wanted to come to your farm. It must have taken a long time to trust she did want to be a friend."

"As I said, about a week. Other kids taunted her about it, but she told them to fuck off in not so many ways. I'd never had a real friend before, so wasn't sure how to act. Didn't wanna scare her off, either. But yeah, when she said she wanted to come to the farm, I was fucking terrified. I didn't really understand what was going on, but subconsciously I knew that what my father was doing to me was wrong, and what if he tried to do it to Gayle as well? I thought I'd be blamed for it and sent to prison. As for my mother, what if we saw her taking a piss in the middle of the farm or hooking up with some guy? Or she was in a bad mood and decided to take it out on us both? I'd lose my new friend immediately, back to square one."

"Tell me about what the other kids used to do and say to you at school."

Claire sighs, as though she really doesn't want to talk about it. As if it upsets her more than discussing the killing and dismemberment of Tania. I find that significant. Strange the things she can talk about freely with not a care in the world, and others cause her certain discomfort. Serial killers and those suffering psychopathy disorders most certainly have their priorities different from the rest.

"From the very first day I started school, I sensed something was wrong. All the other kids had nice, new clothes to wear. Practically fucking sparkling. Not a speck of dirt on them, and there was me wearing torn jeans and trainers. They all soon got together and started playing with each other, and I'd be sitting alone, not knowing what to do. At lunchtime, the kids had fucking delicious sandwiches with chocolate and cake and so on. I had a stale sandwich with maybe one slice of cheese in it and that was that. So there was a sign something wasn't right with me straight away. Didn't change as I grew up either.

"I can remember kids asking me why I wore the same clothes every day. Even then. Why they were torn and my parents didn't buy me new ones. I didn't know what to say; I'd just start crying instead. It was about a year later, as we got older, around six I suppose, when the real bullying started.

"One kid in particular, Jimmy was his name. I remember even now. He was a total arsehole. Him and his friends. Everyone was scared of him. I wouldn't be surprised if he ended up in prison as well, for murder or something. First, they would start by grabbing my measly fucking sandwich and throwing it away when I was already starving. Seeing me cry, they found it hilarious not knowing I wouldn't eat again until that night. If I was lucky.

"From there it progressed. One day I opened my lunchbox, took out my sandwich, and bit into it. Jimmy and his cronies were snickering. I soon found out why. My sandwich tasted funny, all gooey, like

35

some shitty tasting jam inside. But when I opened it and looked, there were two dead worms in it. I'd bitten them in half and swallowed it. The kid found it hilarious.

"Another time, I was sitting alone on the playing field. It was hot, and sometimes they'd let us sit outside at lunch time. I'd only just started eating my sandwich when they all turned up, stupid sly grins on their faces, but there was something in their eyes which worried me. Something I didn't like. Jimmy nudged his friend, this fat fuck, all greasy hair and acne. They were older than me, see. "Sandwich nice, pig?" he asks. I said nothing. Then he comes over, his hand is behind his back so he's obviously hiding something. He squats beside me and asks me if I'd like some extra filling in my sandwich. I told him to go away and leave me alone. He didn't like that, so he slaps me across the face and grabs my sandwich.

"'Hey, give it back!' I plead, already in tears like a stupid, little baby. He brings out this bag he had hidden in his hand and emptied the contents into my sandwich. It was a lump of dog shit. 'Eat it,' he says, but before I could throw it away and run to tell the teachers, he grips my hand in his so I can't drop the sandwich and says, 'eat it or I'm gonna smear it all over your face and up your pussy and tell everyone you did it yourself.' But still I refused. I tried to scream for help, but before I could, he pinches my cheeks, forcing my mouth open, then shoves the sandwich inside. 'Fucking eat it, you fucking pig, or I'm gonna cut your face open.' Then he brings out a little penknife and holds the blade against my eyeball. So I ate it. Every little piece until I threw up. They burst out laughing, found it hysterical. For the next two days, all I could taste in my mouth was dog shit. I could smell it everywhere, and when I got home that night, my mother sent me to bed with no supper because I threw up on my top and it stained it. She wouldn't even listen when I tried to explain why. This and other things went on nearly every day until Jimmy got expelled for fighting."

This is the most tragic thing I have ever heard. Can anyone really blame her for the way she turned out?

"What are your thoughts on Jimmy now? I'm surprised you didn't track him down."

"Oh, I had every intention of doing so. I was going to kidnap him and make him eat his own shit until he choked on it. I heard about someone doing that. Some detective made these guys eat this soup with their own shit in it. That must have been funny as fuck, but I guess I'll never get the chance. Shame that."

Chapter 5

Jean and Kenny had been married for fifteen years. Claire was dragged from Jean's womb as an unexpected and unwanted gift, like receiving a visit from a police officer with bad news. Neither of them had wanted to have kids. They both detested kids in equal amounts. Too noisy, too demanding, and more importantly, too expensive to maintain. Before they had inherited the farm and lake, money had already been tight, almost to the point of non-existent. Jean didn't work because she said it was a man's job to do such things while the wife stayed at home, the idea being a faithful housewife, but the only thing she was faithful to was legal and illegal substances.

The only time the small bungalow they were living in at the time saw a broom or a mop was if they had visitors. These times were very rare instances either of their parents or Jean's sister, Carol, decided to make a visit. And even then, it was a bare necessities situation, just enough to look like she'd made an effort. Because she didn't really give a shit what they said anyway. If bored, she might wash the dishes if there was no more room in the sink or replace the overflowing rubbish bag with a new one, leaving the filled one in the unkept back garden.

Once wedding rings were exchanged, she stopped worrying about herself too. Not that she cared too much, anyway, but appearances had to be kept if she was to find someone who was going to fund lifestyle and keep a roof over her head. Jean had never worked a day in her life and had no intentions of doing so. She stopped watching what she ate, and soon the clothes she wore were too small. Makeup was abandoned, also meaning her previously fair complexion soon became blotchy from eating so much junk food, and there was a perpetual redness on her nose and cheeks from drinking cheap wine. Her once long, blonde hair was now cut short and greasy, tangles common from lack of brushing. Where her eyes had once been a bright blue, something Claire had inherited, they were now perpetually bloodshot. Her fingers were stained a dark yellow from having a cigarette in her hand at all times, and her teeth were going the same way. And whenever Kenny reflected on the fact that his wife was now a fat, ugly bitch, she told him that if he didn't like it, he could happily fuck off back to his parents. She'd soon find someone else to take his place and more importantly pay the mortgage.

She may have been the poorest girl in class, everyone avoided her and taunted her, but Jean wasn't stupid. She learned to use her wits and bigger build to manipulate the other girls. When she needed the answers to exam results, because she never once did her homework and her parents never checked, either, she would threaten the cleverer girls. If that didn't work, she would wait for them outside after school and hit them where no marks would be left or, even better, follow them home then tell them if they didn't comply, she'd burn their house down in the middle of the night. That always worked.

As she grew into a teen, she understood how to manipulate the boys too. A short skirt, show off an already ample bosom, promises of a blowjob in the toilets, and they would do whatever she wanted. At fifteen, she was already letting them do what they wanted according to how much they were willing to pay. It was a lesson she never forgot. And this was how she met Kenny.

When both were sixteen, Kenny was already working, which suggested to Jean that here was someone who would be able to maintain her lifestyle forever. He was well-built, over six feet tall already, and had strong, firm muscles from working on a building site as a labourer. Curly, black hair, chestnut-coloured eyes, a prominent jaw, and big, strong hands, she fell for him immediately, especially as he seemed shy and reserved when they spoke. Anytime she mentioned how cute and handsome he looked, he would blush and get tongue-tied. He didn't get tongue-tied when he went down on her for the first time, though, and he certainly wasn't reserved when they fucked, which soon became every day. He had everything she looked for in a future husband: a job, good, boyish looks, and between his legs was more than enough to keep her satisfied. They were already living in the bungalow three months after their first date. A year later they were married, and she had him in her clutches. But, just when Jean thought she had everything under control, Kenny out working every day and already developing a sizeable beer gut, along came Claire.

She didn't even know she was pregnant until a few months later, assuming the growing stomach was due to her preference for junk food. When she finally had to go to the doctors with stomach pains and was given the news, her first thought had been an abortion. But it was too late for that now. Her next thought was to give it up for adoption, and she made the necessary moves to do so, but it turned out to be just as complicated. She even thought of just dumping the newborn baby on someone's doorstep and letting them worry about her, but the last thing she wanted was to get arrested. By the time Claire was a year old and still she hadn't been taken off Jean's hands, she gave up on the idea.

She hated every second of it. As she had known would be the case, having to wake up every three hours at night during the first few months to feed her was a living hell. She even considered trying to set up a drip feed so Claire was never hungry, but the logistics were too complicated. Besides, the baby needed its nappy changed every now and again too. The very expensive nappy. To avoid wasting good money on nappies, she used towels instead. Jean only ever attended to Claire when she was crying and, even then, only when it was clear Claire wasn't going to miraculously shut up. Several times when Jean was drunk and awoken during the night to attend to her daughter, she considered drowning the baby in the bathtub or just taking her somewhere and abandoning her, but as before, if social workers enquired about her, she would be in trouble. However, sometimes when drunk and the baby was crying incessantly, Jean liked to stub her cigarettes out on the baby's behind, where no one would see it. She'd laugh at Claire's screaming, telling her that at least she now had reason to cry. She would heat Claire's milk so that it was almost boiling then drip it into her open mouth. And when Claire was really howling non-stop for what seemed like hours, she would take Claire's soiled towel and smear the dirty contents all over her face and in her mouth, leaving her like it all day until Kenny was due home from work.

And if Jean had absolutely no emotional attachment to Claire, Kenny had much less. He came home from work each night, sat in front of the TV with an endless supply of beer, and fell asleep. Except for the times when, even then, she would find him cuddled next to Claire in bed, both of them naked.

When the baby woke him, the arguing would ensue, Kenny telling Jean to shut the stupid thing up. From the moment Claire was born, arguing and fighting would be a constant, always about the same things—money and an unwanted child ruining their sleep and life. Then, Kenny's grandparents died in a car accident, and for some reason, instead of leaving the farm and all the ground to Kenny's parents, they had left it to Kenny. It seemed their financial problems were over. But with the stress of running the farm, ensuring the lake was always stocked with fish and clean, came Jean's need for more drugs and alcohol, and Claire was getting bigger which meant she needed clothes and supplies for school. They were earning more money from the fishermen and from what they made on the farm, but it took more work from both of them to keep it that way. Even if it only meant going around the lake three times a day to collect money from the fishermen, it was three times too many as far as Jean was concerned.

"Instead of your fat ass on the sofa most of the day or fucking them pigs or whatever you do with them, you could collect the money from the fishermen! I don't see why I have to do it. It's your fucking lake, not mine," she yelled at him one afternoon.

"Because you don't do fuck all else all day. Sitting there on *your* fat arse eating biscuits and cake all day, watching that crap on TV. Look at you, you look like my grandmother!"

"Fuck you! Your dinner don't cook itself. Your clothes don't wash themselves. Your daughter don't feed herself. I ain't got time to go all the way around the lake."

"Bullshit. My dinner don't cook itself or my clothes wash themselves 'cause I have to do that too. As for your daughter, she might as well be abandoned. You're a fuckin' shit mother and wife. And I don't see you complaining when you go bring one of them fishermen back here to fuck all afternoon. What, you think I don't know?"

"Fuck you! If you weren't such a fat fuck, I might be able to find your little dick under all the fuckin' blubber. I got needs too."

She picked up an ashtray and threw it at him. Claire watched and listened, scared, from the hallway as they argued in the living room. She'd only just got home from school, and they hadn't heard her come in.

The ashtray hit Kenny on the side of the face, too slow to react. Jean laughed.

Kenny glared at her, his face even more red than normal, panting heavily, his hands clenching into fists. "You fuckin' bitch." He grabbed the heavy glass ashtray and threw it back. Jean stepped aside and easily missed it. It landed on the floor and smashed in two. She retaliated by throwing a porcelain vase at him, a wedding present from his parents. Again, he was too slow to react. It hit him in the mouth, his lips exploding, blood running down his chest. He spat out a thick, crimson wad and wiped his mouth, smearing his face. Then, he charged her, arm pulled back ready to punch her. But while Jean was also overweight, Kenny was far more so, and it was easy for Jean to dodge his advances, dancing around the table as he spat and swore at her, trying to hit her. On the second time around the table, Jean quickly bent down and picked up one half of the broken ashtray. When Kenny lashed out at her, she brought the sharp edge of the ashtray down on his arm. A long, deep gash leaked more blood.

Claire was terrified, convinced they were going to kill each other and by the sight of so much blood. She'd never seen as much on a person before. She opened her mouth to scream but was incapable of articulating any sound. Her parents were completely unaware she was there, anyway, and wouldn't have stopped if they saw her. This was by no means the first time she heard them arguing and fighting, but it was the first time she saw so much blood.

"I'm gonna fuckin' kill ya, that's what I'm gonna do!" he screamed, spraying crimson everywhere. Jean responded by laughing at him, jeering and cackling.

"You can't even kill a fuckin' chicken properly, so what you gonna do to me?"

"Fuckin' strangle ya, that's what I'll do."

He was panting even harder now, sweat running down his face, mingling with the blood and leaving trails. He looked like a warrior wearing war paint. But now, instead of trying to run around the table and grab her, he threw the wooden table against the wall, where it shattered. He charged her.

Even so, he completely missed the other half of

the ashtray on the floor, stepped on it, and his feet were taken out from under him. He landed heavily on his back, his head crashing against the floor, and he lay there semi-conscious. Jean went and stood over him then spat on his face, sneering at her husband.

"You useless, fat piece of shit. If it wasn't for having to feed the animals as well, I'd fuckin' kill ya right where you are and cash in on the life insurance."

She punted him between the legs. Kenny groaned and rolled over.

It was the first time Claire subconsciously associated women not necessarily being the weaker sex physically and that words could be just as deadly and powerful as a fist.

Chapter 6

The summer holidays came. For Claire, it was a bittersweet time. On the one hand, she was glad to be away from the bullies and the other kids that taunted her. She wouldn't have to search through piles of dirty clothes for what smelled the least bad or wasn't too grimy. She wouldn't have to sit and watch the other kids eating their mid-morning snacks or at dinnertime huddled together with mouths full and laughing while she had meagre offerings to eat. A sandwich that was practically devoid of any fillings and an apple if she was lucky. If her father remembered to check the apple trees near the farm and they weren't filled with maggots. On the other hand, it also meant she would miss her one and only friend, Gayle.

After what happened with her father, Gayle had burst out crying, scared by his actions, and demanded to phone her mother. She promised Claire she wouldn't say anything, but she also said she didn't want to come back there anymore. And besides, Gayle and her family were going down to Cornwall to visit relations for a while. So once again, Claire was alone, trapped in a home where she was unwanted, uncared for, unloved. It was going to be a long summer.

Given that her parents didn't care where she was, and after the big fight before, Claire wasn't so sure she wanted to be with them either. She spent most of her days out of the house, weather permitting. Even on the days it was drizzly or raining, which for eastern England was often, she still found reason to go for walks. She had a tattered, waterproof jacket in her wardrobe, which was now too small for her, but after a little struggling, she managed to fit into it and the hood more or less covered her head. If she came home soaking wet, her mother would slap her for dirtying the already dirty floors, but she always made sure to take off her leaking boots and her coat first. If she had the capabilities, she would have made a sandwich for herself and not return for lunch at all. Her mother often forgot to make lunch, anyway, so everyone would have to fend for themselves regardless. It was her father who usually left her an extra plate of whatever leftovers he could find, while her mother snored on the sofa or watched TV. Doing the rounds three times a day at the lake was tiring, she said.

As she gained confidence, she would walk farther and farther, bored with seeing the same trees, fields, and animals. She dreamed of going on an adventure to some magical place where McDonalds and KFC and Burger King gave away the food for free, along with free Coca Colas. Claire had only ever been to each place once when she was younger, and kids from school held parties there, parents insisting all kids were invited. She thought it was the tastiest food in the world. She would eat nothing but burgers and fried chicken if she had the chance. She wanted to meet other children who would all be her best friends, and she would have magical parents that would spoil her with all the best clothes, the games consoles, Nike trainers, tracksuits, t-shirts, jackets, everything. Claire would have a dog, too, a golden retriever that would follow her everywhere and never leave her side. Even at night.

While on these journeys, she would edge closer and closer to what was her nearest neighbour. They had a cottage with a thatched roof, and there was always a green jeep parked in the driveway. Sometimes she would sit and watch to see if anyone came out, too shy to get any closer and introduce herself. Her mother was constantly telling her she was a horrible little girl that no one loved and everyone hated and she was an embarrassment to them. She didn't know why, because as far as she knew she hadn't done anything to upset her parents, but if her mother kept saying it was true, she assumed that somehow it must be. It was another reason she didn't want to get too close, in case she frightened them and they made her run away. Today, though, she felt more confident. It was warm and sunny, and this made her feel happier than usual.

Claire sat a little farther down from the cottage, beside the winding road. She hoped they had a dog they might let her stroke and play with. She'd always wanted a dog, but her parents said they were too expensive to maintain and would attack the animals. She sat there for a long time and was thinking about going home when the front door opened. A woman stepped out, rubbing her belly. She was pregnant. Then a man stepped out, followed by a boy about her age but who didn't go to her school. All three were laughing and joking, which almost brought tears to Claire's eyes. In that moment, she was jealous. She wanted to run over to them and hug the two adults, pretend they were her parents instead.

The man opened the passenger door of the Jeep, and the woman was about to step in when she happened to glance in Claire's direction. Her smile wavered and she frowned. She said something to the man, and then all three were looking at her, confused expressions on their faces. After a couple of minutes talking quietly among themselves, all three came over to Claire.

"Hey! Are you lost?" asked the woman as she squatted beside her.

Claire shook her head. The man stood beside who Claire assumed to be his wife, while the boy glared at her from behind his father.

"No. I live farther down. At the lake."

"Oh, I know the place. Green Lake. And what are you doing out here by yourself? Are your parents about?"

"No, they're at home. I go for walks sometimes when I'm bored. Is that a baby inside you?"

"Well, yes, what a clever girl. Are you sure your parents won't be worried you're so far from home on your own? What's your name?"

"I'm Claire. No, they don't care. Most of the time they don't even know I'm gone. Mum's usually asleep on the sofa or watching TV. Then she has to collect money from the fishermen. And dad is always with the pigs and the animals, feeding them and stuff."

The couple looked at each other dubiously. The man shrugged.

"Well, I'm Kathleen, this is my husband, Martin, and our son, Michael. You know, I'm sure they do care, but they must be very busy running the lake and farm. I'm not sure they'd like it if they knew you were this far from home on your own. How old are you, Claire?"

"I'm seven now. And it's true, they told me they

don't care. Most of the time they don't even know I'm gone. Can I touch it?"

"I'm sorry. What?"

"Your belly. Can I touch it?"

"Oh! Well, yeah, sure."

Kathleen stood up and moved closer to Claire, who timidly placed her hand on Kathleen's belly. "When will it be born?"

"Well, she will be born in about three months' time. It's a girl."

"Nice. I wish I had a sister. It gets lonely being on my own."

"Aww, that's sad. Maybe one day you'll have a brother or sister. But listen, why don't we drive you back home? It will start getting dark soon, and I'm really sure your parents will start to worry. And look, Michael is often bored too. You could come to our house and play if you like some time. With your parent's permission, of course."

"Could I? Really?!"

"Sure! He's got the new PlayStation and games on his computer, too, so I'm sure there'll be something you can play!"

A groan came from behind Martin. Michael glared at his mother, who ignored it.

"Sure thing!" said Martin. "Michael drives us nuts hanging around us all day. It'll be nice for him to make some new friends. Right, buddy?"

"Yeah, sure, Dad."

Despite the fact Claire was overjoyed and excited at the prospect of having a new friend and finally getting to play games, there was also another feeling inside her. One she knew even better.

Jealousy.

***

For a child to feel unloved by their own parents is truly a terrible thing. The worst thing. Children need to feel loved and wanted to develop into empathetic adults later. From the moment Claire was born, she must have sensed, on some subconscious level, she was an unwanted child.

"Is there a moment when you thought to yourself that perhaps you were an unwanted child? That you were a burden to your family? Perhaps an inciting moment, something defining?"

"Oh, from my earliest memories. My dad was already sticking his cock in my mouth, remember, when I was a baby. But I understood that for different reasons, obviously, until I was older. My mother though…From the moment she spat me out I think I knew.

"I remember being spanked or slapped every time I cried or said I was hungry. That must have been when I was about three or four. Sometimes, just trying to give her a hug she'd push me away and tell me to leave her alone. Once I tried to sit on her lap because I wanted a cuddle and accidently knocked her cigarette on the cushion, burning a hole. She went fucking apeshit, picked up the smouldering cigarette and stubbed it out on the palm of my hand then told me not to fucking touch her ever again. I screamed.

"On the rare occasions she would cook, I'd go into the kitchen and compliment her on how wonderful it was, because, like, back then, of course, I was looking for ways for her to like me, say nice things to me. I just wanted to please her so she would be happy, because I'm telling myself it must be my fault. I'm stupid, clumsy, and it's my fault for making her angry. So, she's cooking some stew, and I dipped a finger in it and licked it and made these noises suggesting how wonderful it was, and I told her she was a great cook and I wish I could grow up to be as good as her.

"This stew was boiling, obviously. Bubbling away. She grabbed my hand and shoved it into the stew. My whole hand, and she left it there for about ten seconds, me howling in agony. She tells me I ever do it again, she would shove my whole face in it. When she pulled my hand out, it was red raw and blistering, the skin peeling in places already. Then, she gets the wooden spoon she was using to stir the stew, dips it into the pot and flicks the boiling liquid at my face. Some of it went in my eye. I couldn't see properly for the rest of the day. As a further punishment, at dinner time she made me sit at the table while she and dad ate it and I wasn't allowed. I had to sit and watch and when they'd finished— every last morsel—I was sent to bed hungry. I think I was about five at the time, and it was then I kinda realised my mother was never going to love me no matter what I did."

"That is sick, Claire. Truly sick. Your mother should never have been allowed to keep you. Maybe everything could have been avoided had that happened."

"Yeah, well, too late now, innit? The biggest shame is she died from natural causes, because if not, I would have cooked her in her own stew. Bit by bit so she was still alive to eat herself."

"And your father never did anything to stop the abuse?"

She snorts.

"Fuck he did. He was scared of her too. And probably thought that if the abuse was reported I'd be put into care, and where was he gonna stick his dick at nights?"

Chapter 7

Claire said nothing to her parents about her neighbours or having a new friend to play with. She knew they wouldn't care, anyway, but she wanted to keep it a secret, like a new toy to be kept hidden so no one else could play with it. She had gone so long without having friends, Gayle aside, that she felt as though by telling people about Michael and his parents they might be taken from her. And that wasn't going to happen. Michael was hers and hers alone.

The very next day after meeting them she returned, practically running to their cottage almost as soon as she'd finished breakfast. Michael's mother looked a little surprised to see her so early in the day but let her in and showed her to Michael's room. He, too, looked more than a little surprised and annoyed as well; it was clear to Claire he wasn't as eager as his parents at the prospect of having a girl around the place. But Michael must have been raised well, because he said nothing and allowed Claire to play games on his computer. When lunch time came, Claire reluctantly said she had to go home, but Kathleen must have spotted the disappointment on her face because she invited Claire to stay for lunch with the two of them, Martin being at work. Claire's face lit up.

"But we won't get into trouble with your mother, will we? I mean, if she's already prepared lunch and you don't turn up, she might get annoyed. Maybe I should phone her to let her know."

"No, don't. It's okay. She won't mind," she said quickly.

Kathleen didn't appear entirely convinced but said nothing. When lunch was brought out, steak and chips, Claire was almost drooling. Her stomach rumbled, as though she hadn't eaten in days, and she had to force herself to eat slowly so as not to give away how hungry and desperate she was. And when chocolate ice cream was brought out afterwards, she nearly cried. She couldn't recall the last time she'd eaten any. As the afternoon passed and Michael seemed more accepting of her, Kathleen had to keep hinting to Claire that it was getting late and she really should be heading home soon. After the third reminder, Kathleen refused to take no for an answer and drove her home, leaving her at the entrance to the grounds. Before she turned around and drove off, she told Claire she could come any time she liked, which the girl took full advantage of. For the next four days, she appeared on their doorstep at the same time and stayed until she was told it was time to go home. By now, even Michael treated her as a friend.

And yet, the disappointment at having to go back to the farm was huge. Claire wanted to stay and live with them. When she did go home, neither of her parents asked her where she'd been all day, so surely they wouldn't care if she moved in permanently. But there was another aspect that Claire didn't like—the kisses and hugs from Michael's parents to their son but not for her. The way Kathleen would tickle him, make him laugh, joke with him. Michael would lay his head on his mother's belly and speak to his new sister, leaving Claire alone and feeling left out. But the most devastating thing occurred on the fifth day. Kathleen told Claire she couldn't come the next day because the three of them were going away for the

weekend and wouldn't be back until late Sunday
night. But when Claire went to their house anyway
Saturday afternoon, hiding behind a hedgerow and
saw them moving about in the house, and again on
Sunday, she knew she had been tricked. They had
lied to her to stop her from visiting. In her young
mind, she was being abandoned yet again.

Claire spent the evening in her room, but she had
an idea. Maybe she was being too insistent with them
and they were getting fed up with having her around
the house all day. If she brought Michael here, it
would make a change from being at his all the time.
They could play a game. If he enjoyed it so much, he
might tell his parents how cool Claire was, and they
wouldn't lie to her again. She was still upset about
that and was convinced it had been Michael who told
his parents to make her stay away. She'd teach him.

After visiting their home Monday afternoon and
pretending to be ignorant of their deceit, Michael was
allowed to come to the farm the next day. Claire
couldn't wait. She waited at the entrance to the farm
after lunch, as agreed, and was buzzing with
excitement when the jeep came down the dirt track,
kicking up dust. Her parents were both indoors,
asleep after another argument. Claire didn't tell them
about Michael visiting in case they said no. They
wouldn't be bothering the two kids all afternoon
anyway. Kathleen told Michael she'd be back to
fetch him at six, then left.

"Wow, this place is huge!" said Michael, wide-
eyed and looking around. "I wanna go fishing on the
lake."

"Tell your dad to buy a fishing rod and you can!
But first, you wanna see the animals?"

"Yeah!"

Like Gayle, Michael was in awe of them all, being able to get so close to them, touch them in many cases, although the geese didn't appear to be so happy about it, one of them chasing after him for a while, which Claire found hilarious. Then they went to the pig pens.

"Wow, they're huge! Do they bite?"

"No. They're really friendly. I used to have names for all of them, but not anymore. They used to eat corn out of my hand, too, like the ducks and chickens," she lied.

There were conflicting feelings in her mind right now that her young brain was incapable of interpreting correctly. On the one hand, she wanted both her and Michael to be friends, and she wanted to impress him so he thought she was cool; but on the other, that he had surely told his mother to lie to her, stop her from coming over at the weekend, was painful and humiliating. She wanted him to know what it was to feel hurt and suffering too. Why should it just be her that lived an unloved life? It wasn't fair.

"You could do the same you know. Sometimes I play a game. See how long I can stay in a pen before the smell makes me leave. Like a test we do at school. You wanna play? They won't hurt you."

He looked dubiously at the pigs, snorting and grunting as they shuffled around in circles. The dark male was up on its hind legs watching them, its beady eyes bloodshot like Claire's parents almost always were.

"I dunno," said Michael slowly. "That one looks nasty. What if it bit me?"

"Why would it bite you? They eat potatoes and corn and stuff, not meat! Are you scared of a pig? You must be the only person in the whole world that's scared of a pig! I've been in there loads of times."

"I'm not scared. I just…they smell."

"You're lying! You're scared. My dad cleaned out the pens this morning, so they don't even smell bad yet. I'm gonna tell my friend Gayle you're scared of a little pig!"

"I'm not scared! Don't you tell anyone. Okay, I'll do it. But not that one," he said pointing to the boar.

"Okay, that one then," she said pointing to another. This was the biggest sow of them all. Claire had an idea it was pregnant. Michael still looked dubious but agreed. Claire opened the gate and stepped aside.

Michael edged his way in, still unsure of himself, keeping to the edge of the pen. The sow grunted and stepped back. Claire quickly closed the gate as soon as Michael was in, virtually shoving him inside, then locked it.

"See, she doesn't bite. Now you have to stand at the back and see how brave you are."

"I don't like it anymore. I wanna come out."

"You've only just gone in. You're scared! You have to stay there until your mum comes back."

"No way! That's hours. I wanna get out. Let me out."

"No."

She watched as the sow started grunting louder, sniffing the air, getting more nervous. Its grunts were faster, practically growling like a dog. Michael was pressed hard against the brick wall, too high for him to climb up, and besides, behind the pen was where her dad dumped all the waste when cleaning. Claire knew it was almost knee high in pig shit and old straw. Bugs and beetles lived there in the hundreds.

The sow took a step closer, clearly agitated. Claire was holding her breath, a grin on her face. Michael looked like he was about to burst out crying at any second. It sniffed Michael's legs, opened its mouth, and grunted even louder than before.

"Please, I wanna get out. Open the gate."

"No."

The sow opened its huge mouth and nipped at Michael's jeans. If the pig reared up on its hind legs it would have towered over him. If Michael slipped and it lay on him, he would be instantly crushed. He started crying.

"Please, let me out. Help!" he yelled.

"If you shout, you'll make it worse."

The sow snorted then made to bite him again. A wet patch appeared at his groin, and this time Claire did open the gate.

"Quick. You got two seconds before I close it again."

Michael wasted no time and ran, almost tripping over his feet as he did so. He ran away from the pens while Claire laughed hysterically.

"It was just a game. I was gonna let you out soon as you came over. You wet yourself. I'm gonna tell Gayle that, too, when we go back to school."

"I wanna go home. Call my mum. The pig was gonna eat me and you knew! You did it on purpose."

"I didn't. I was just playing. Pigs don't bite. It was just a game."

But inside, Claire was laughing. That would teach

him to lie to her. This was another lesson Claire learned.

Manipulation of others.

Revenge.

Chapter 8

Somehow, Claire's mother discovered she had been going to the nearest neighbour's house on a regular basis. She was furious. She wanted nothing to do with any neighbours and much less her daughter visiting them. When she found out Michael had even been on the premises, Claire went three days without supper and was forced to clean the whole house from top to bottom, scrubbing the floors with a filthy rag until they were spotless. She spent the rest of the summer locked in her bedroom. A bucket was left in the corner of the room for her to use when she needed the toilet. Her food was brought to her once a day, whatever leftovers were laying about, be it cold soup or soggy vegetables. The whole time she was locked in her room—three months almost—she wasn't allowed to shower, not once. She spent many nights crying herself to sleep and spent the days huddled in bed, alone with her thoughts and the smell of her waste from the bucket, which her mother emptied once a day, and the acrid smell of her own sweat and filth. Her father still visited on a regular basis but did nothing to help her, slipping in and out of her room late at night.

Until now, she had always believed everything was her fault, that no matter how hard she tried she kept messing up somehow, saying or doing the wrong thing to upset her parents. That they must be really tired running the lake and the farm, and because they never had enough money to buy things, never had the time to do things together, but now she was beginning to learn this wasn't the case. There was no reason to punish her this way for visiting Michael each day. If anything, she had been keeping out of their way and letting them have their afternoon naps, not begging and pleading for food because she was hungry—the times she spent the day at Michael's, she ate with them. For the first time in her short life, she came to fully understand that no matter what she did or didn't do, her parents simply didn't love her. Not like Michael's parents loved him, or Gayle's parents, or the other kids at school whose parents were waiting for them after school with smiles and treats and snacks. And regardless of what Claire said or did, nothing was ever going to change it.

If asked to explain what it meant, she would have been incapable, but a therapist would have used the word resentment to describe what was going through her mind as she spent that claustrophobic summer shut in her room. She wasn't even allowed to open the window; her mother nailed it shut should Claire get it in her head to sneak out. The room was stuffy, like being locked in a wardrobe, and she often screamed and howled to be let out, but it made no difference. To pass the time, she drew on the walls, read the same books over and over, lay on her bed and fantasised some more about her magical land. She couldn't understand why Michael hadn't come looking for her, or his parents; surely, they must have found it strange she never returned to their cottage? After the event with the pig, Claire promised she wouldn't say anything to anyone, and Michael agreed not to tell his parents. He was embarrassed to admit he'd wet himself, anyway, but he did tell Claire she could come back any time. But no one came looking for her. She might as well have been dead, she figured.

No one loved her, no one cared about her, much less her parents, especially her mother. She began to think of her in a different light, replaying in her mind all the times she'd punished Claire; hitting her with various tools and implements across the arms, legs, and buttocks; forcing her to go to school with filthy, smelly clothes; starving her. One time when Claire wouldn't stop crying because she was hungry, her mother forced her to smoke a cigarette. The smoke hurt her lungs so much and made her so nauseous, instead of crying, she spent the next fifteen minutes vomiting, her throat too sore to cry anymore. Claire had to clean it all up with her bare hands. Only her father paid her attention, and it was for his personal benefit. When she woke up in the morning her body ached in places it shouldn't, and somehow she knew it was her father's doing. The world was out to hurt Claire for no reason at all, and it wasn't fair. It wasn't fair at all.

She had no notion of time when her mother came into her room one morning and told her to get up and go shower. She didn't know if three months had passed or three years. But her initial reaction was that her mother was finally relenting and ending her punishment.

"Get up. School starts today. And get showered. You stink and look like shit. I don't want the social services on my case as well. You got twenty minutes."

She threw a pile of clean clothes at her and left.

Claire was shocked. She hadn't a clue it was school already. All concept of time had vanished along with her hopes of ever making her parents love her like the other kids. She sat up, stared at the pile of clothes for a while, then made her way to the shower. She cried as she allowed the lukewarm water to run over her body, finally, to wash her hair that was in greasy clumps. For the first time, she was glad to go to school. Fresh air, finally allowed to leave this room and stretch her legs properly, reunite with Gayle. Ask Michael why he hadn't come looking for her if he was going to be stationed at the same school as her. Run and play and be free. Maybe even run away from home and never return.

The feel of the warm water on her skin was bliss. For three months she had felt like the pigs in their pens, rolling around in her own filth. That day, Michael had complained about the smell; if he had come anywhere near her just ten minutes ago, he would have died from intoxication. She covered herself in a plentiful supply of gel and shampoo for her hair, which had grown considerably, and breathed in the aroma of the gels, imagining herself to be running wild in a field full of flowers. It was only when her mother yelled at her to turn the fucking water off right now that she stopped. She could have happily stood there all day. She dressed and headed downstairs, looking forward to the day ahead for the first time in months.

"Next time you waste that much water, I'll fuckin' drown you in it," spat her mother as she threw a packed lunch box at her. "You think water's free or what? Fuckin' girl, no good for nuffin'. Only makin' me spend money. Go on, get out."

The smile left her face again, replaced by the threat of tears. She wished she had the courage to ask her mother why she hated her so but knew it would only end up with her getting slapped or pushed out the door. So she said nothing and headed down the track to wait for the bus. Her sadness was soon replaced by smiles again, though, as the fresh air blew around her, birds chirping as they flew overhead, things she had taken for granted for so long but had been cruelly taken from her. She would never take anything for granted ever again she told herself as she waited for the bus to pull up. When it arrived and she saw familiar faces, the last three months of imprisonment were almost forgotten. She saw Gayle sitting near the back, and they were soon busily chatting about their adventures over the summer, although Claire said nothing about her punishment. It was later in the day that she would think of it again.

She was sitting with Gayle chatting when three older boys came over, smirks on their faces.

"Well, look who it is," said one. "The farm girl. What's the matter, too busy playing with pigs to get a haircut? Do you sleep with them? Play with them? 'Cause you look like one."

The other kids burst out laughing.

"Shut up," she said.

"Shut up? You gonna make me, pig girl? Do you make oinking sounds when you're in there with 'em? Do you...do things with 'em?"

The kids sniggered.

"Are their dicks like their tails, all curly? You should know, little piggie."

"Leave us alone. You're stupid!"

"You smell like 'em too. Do you fuck 'em, piggie? Rub their little dicks and make 'em squirt? I bet you do. I bet you love it, don't yer? Lying there all naked with the piggies when they do stuff to yer."

Some primal feeling that had been lying dormant awoke. She wasn't entirely sure of what they were implying or saying, but the mention of being touched where she shouldn't be caused her nerves to flare, for a sudden rage to make her tremble. In that moment, she wanted to hurt this kid very badly, him and his friends, and if she had had anything resembling a weapon with her, she might have done so. She thought of the way her mother had defended herself against her dad, so much bigger than mum. Claire stood up and faced the boy, perhaps two years older than she was.

"I bet the pig's dicks are bigger than yours. I bet you got a little peanut for a dick and you're jealous and you can't even find it when you go to the toilet."

The kid's face turned red. His friends laughed hysterically, surely never believing a seven-year-old girl would be able to return the insults in such a way.

"You stupid, smelly, poor, little bitch. With your fucking hand-me-down clothes. You're a fucking freak. You should die. You're no good for nuffin'."

The way he looked at her, the way he spoke, reminded her of her mother, and Claire had had enough. With Gayle begging her to just walk away, Claire did the opposite. She took a step back and kicked him between the legs. The kid crumpled.

The other two kids stopped laughing and stared gobsmacked at Claire, backing away slowly. The kid on the ground was wincing, tears running down his cheeks but unable to cry because it appeared the wind had been taken from him. He rolled around clutching his damaged groin while Claire stood over him. Other kids had seen what happened because they all came running over, gasping and laughing.

For the first time, Claire felt something resembling control in her life. She had single-handedly taken care of the bully without any help from anyone, and she felt the power coursing through her. It must be how her mother felt when retaliating against her dad. The other kids jostled around in a circle, expectant, guessing a fight was about to take place, and Claire was enjoying the attention for once, until a couple of girls started insulting her.

"You're a freak, you know that?"

"Is that what you do to the animals on the farm? Bully and kick them?"

"You're sick. He was only joking."

"I bet your mum and dad hit you as well, don't they? That's where you learned how to do that."

"You're a bully and stupid. You should go back to your stinky farm and stay there. We don't want you here. You don't even wear new clothes or anything. Your family are freaks."

Shocked by their reaction, when they knew full well it had been the kid that started on her first, Claire burst out crying and ran off just as a teacher approached, asking what was going on. It seemed no matter what she did, she did it wrong. Both at home and at school. It didn't make any sense. She didn't want to go home, and she didn't want to be here anymore either. Not even Gayle had defended her. Claire seriously considered running away or just wishing she was dead.

Chapter 9

Claire had just got home from school. After kicking the boy, she had been taken to the headmaster's office and asked to explain her actions. All the teachers knew she was often subjected to verbal abuse from the other kids and privately hazarded a guess as to what her living conditions were like at home—they sometimes asked her if things were okay—but the teacher and the headmaster were still shocked about the sudden outburst of violence from her. She told them what the boy had said and that something suddenly came over her and she couldn't help herself. The mention of doing bad things with the pigs had triggered something in her she couldn't explain. But the looks on the teachers' and headmaster's faces suggested they had an idea. She was still surprised, though, when they said they weren't going to inform her parents or expel her from school, only issuing a stern warning that next time she was to tell the teacher. Claire fully agreed.

She was still thinking about how lenient they'd been when she entered the farm grounds. At first, when she saw her mother laughing and giggling with a man, his back to Claire, she thought it was her dad. It made her smile to see her mother finally in a good mood—maybe she'd changed her attitude. But then she saw it wasn't her father she was getting cuddly with, rubbing herself up against him, running her hands over his thighs, but one of the fishermen. Claire hid behind a tree and watched.

"You get any bites today?" she asked, her words

slurring.

"Not a lot, no."

"Well, that's a shame, innit? Perhaps you'd like for something else to bite instead, huh?"

"Oh, yeah? And what are you proposing?"

"Well, you could dangle your bait over my mouth and see if I take it. I can be your fishy. I love to suck on all types of bait."

They both chuckled.

"Well, how could I refuse that? What's your favourite bait?"

"Big, fat worms that go straight to the back of my throat. Can you do that? You got a big, fat worm to tease me with?"

"I'm sure I can come up with something!"

"Mmm! I bet you can come."

Claire watched, horrified and embarrassed, as her mother ran a hand over his crotch, oblivious to the other fishermen around the lake. But that was nothing compared to what happened next.

"Fuck, you're making me all horny. Means I need a piss. Hang on."

She went in front of a tree, lifted her skirt, and squatted. She wasn't wearing any knickers and took a piss in front of the bemused fisherman. Claire thought it was the most embarrassing and disgusting thing she had ever seen. At school, older kids said girls who didn't wear underwear were sluts and whores. She wasn't entirely sure of the significance but knew it meant girls who were dirty. But there was her mother doing exactly what the older kids said. And in front of the man, giggling, not a care in the world.

She recalled seeing her mother doing stuff with

the other guy before, both naked, the man hitting her with the whip, and knew they were probably going to do the same thing. She glanced over at the pig pens and saw her father watching the spectacle too. Claire's mother also saw him and waved before standing up, pulling her skirt back down and taking the fisherman away, back to the house. It was the first time Claire was truly aware of two things: her mother was just like the older kids said at school, and her father was a coward and a wimp, too scared or ashamed to say anything. These thoughts would return to her later in life.

When Claire finally found the courage to go to her room, the same grunts and moans came from her mother's bedroom.

"Harder, fisherman, fuck me harder. You said you had a big, fat worm, I wanna feel it all the way up my arse. Slap me, fucker, slap me hard."

He complied, because there was a loud slapping sound which caused her to yell. The bed springs squealed, the head rest banging rapidly against the wall, both of them panting while she hurled insults at him, telling him to do things Claire didn't understand. Why her mother wanted to be choked by this worm they were talking about she didn't know. Claire covered her ears with her hands, but she could still hear the head rest banging against the wall, her mother's loud yells for more and harder. Claire didn't understand the concept of sex, but she knew it was something mums and dads did. She didn't think this was something normal for her mother to be doing with what was essentially a stranger and not caring if dad heard them or not.

When her mother started telling the guy to do it on

her face, she was totally shocked and bewildered. What on earth she wanted the guy to do on her face Claire couldn't even begin to fathom. Slap her, perhaps? But why? That was painful—Claire knew from experience. Whatever it was, her mother was begging for more as the man groaned loudly. Then there was silence. Shortly afterwards, her mother's bedroom door opened. Curious, Claire dared to open hers and peek out. She regretted it instantly and immediately slammed the door shut again, both for fear of retribution and because it had been highly embarrassing. Her mother and the man were both naked, heading towards the shower, but her mother's face was covered in some substance Claire didn't recognise. It looked like her mother had sneezed and the snot had somehow covered her face and neck. She spent the rest of the afternoon in her room, not even coming out when she heard the fisherman thank her mother and leave. She was beginning to seriously worry about her mother's mental health. It wouldn't be the last time.

Chapter 10

Michael absolutely refused to return to Claire's farm but agreed she could go to his home, even though he didn't seem particularly happy about it. But Claire wasn't about to argue with him now that she had somewhere to go and a new friend to play with. After being locked in her room for nearly three months, seeing her mother doing weird stuff with other men, and her parent's constant, violent fights, the last thing she wanted was to be there. By now, she couldn't care less if Michael liked having her around or not—she was coming regardless.

Kathleen's belly was huge now, almost ready to give birth, and Claire loved placing her hand gently against the belly and waiting to feel the baby kick. Michael's dad, Martin, was around more now, too, to keep an eye on his wife he said, ready for when it was time to rush to the hospital. Sometimes, when she was bored with video games, she would leave Michael in his room and go sit between them on the sofa as they watched TV. She would pretend they were her real parents, cuddling up to them and laughing at their jokes, especially Martin. She really liked him, the complete opposite of her real dad with his slim figure, boyish, curly, black hair and warm, blue eyes. When he smiled, he showed perfectly white teeth, like Claire saw on TV advertisements. He said he was a criminal psychologist. She wasn't completely sure what that meant, but he told her it was learning to understand how a bad person's mind worked. This was something Claire found extremely interesting. She was tempted to tell him about her mother and whether there might be something wrong with her, but again, shame and embarrassment prevented her from saying anything. But more than ever, she wished these were her parents and she could live her forever.

Except for the other things.

The way they always insisted she had to go home when she didn't want to. The way they always seemed more affectionate around Michael than her. Jokes they made among themselves that she didn't understand. Sometimes, Martin would bring toys and things home for Michael but not for her, even when he knew she was there. She felt left out again, a part of something fun and exciting but always on the perimeter, never allowed to participate fully, to take a step closer and be accepted as a complete member of the family. Like a stray cat that will drink from a bowl of milk left out for it but always wanting more and not knowing how to ask. She should have been happy as things were, but like the metaphorical cat, she wanted more. She wanted their full, undivided attention.

One afternoon after finishing school—Michael went to a different one—she went straight to his home and waited as always to be let in. Michael's mother would make her a wonderful sandwich, too, the fillings thick that always took away her constant hunger. She often tried to stay until dinner, as well, but Kathleen or Martin insisted she go home before it got late, even if they did drive her there, just in case. She had been thinking of how she could go about getting more attention and thought she had a way. She found Michael doing his homework in his room. After playing a game on his computer and letting him finish his homework, she stopped playing and turned to him.

"Are you a virgin?"

Michael looked at her, confused. "A what?"

"A virgin. Like do you fuck girls?"

Claire wasn't quite sure what she was saying, but she heard her mother use those words a lot and figured it would trigger Michael into a response.

"No. Girls are stupid. I mean, you're okay, but I don't ever want a girlfriend."

"What about your mum and dad? Do you ever watch them fuck? Does your mum get, like, snot all over her face afterwards? Mine does."

"That's gross."

He thought about it for a moment, obviously having no idea what she was talking about, but before he could reply, she continued.

"Can you hear them in bed when they fuck? Like the bed shaking and them making all funny noises? My mum likes getting slapped. I even saw her being hit by a whip once, and the man's thing was thick and stiff. Have you ever seen your dad's thing?"

"I'm telling my mum."

Before she could stop him, he ran downstairs. Claire grinned. He returned with both his parents looking confused and upset. Kathleen squatted beside her.

"Claire, what have you been saying to Michael? Where did you learn language and things like that?"

She shrugged her shoulders. "I dunno. I was just curious, that's all."

"Is that the kind of thing your mum and dad say?" asked Martin.

"Not my dad so much, but my mum does

sometimes. I just wanted to know."

"Well, that's a very bad thing to say, Claire," said Kathleen. "I think I should speak to your mother about that. You can't go around saying such bad things. It's rude and disgusting. I'm very shocked by your behaviour, Claire. If you're going to carry on like that, maybe you shouldn't come anymore."

Inside, Claire was laughing. She had what she wanted—their attention. They were worried about her. They cared about her. Maybe they even loved her.

"I'm sorry! I didn't mean to. I...I didn't know. Please don't tell my mum or stop me from coming. I won't say it again, I promise."

"Okay, apology accepted, but I think it's time for you to go home anyway. It's getting late. C'mon, I'll drive you."

Claire didn't want to go home. She wanted to suck as much affection and attention out of them as she could, like a leech. But the look on the parents' faces suggested she shouldn't push it. Tomorrow she could play some more on their emotions. She knew now what she had to do.

When she arrived home, she groaned when she heard the glass smashing in the living room, elevated voices yelling at each other. She had been planning on asking what was for supper but decided against it. She went to her bedroom instead, anticipating going to bed hungry again and wondering if Michael had ever been hungry before. There was another loud crash; the floor shook as though something huge had just smashed into the ceiling below. She heard her mother screaming something, her father barely audible. Claire wondered if she had hit him again and he was lying on the floor hurt. Fortunately, the banging and yelling stopped, but a few seconds later there came a series of thuds on the stairs—someone was coming up. Claire braced herself, praying her mother was just going to the toilet or, even better, bed.

Her bedroom door flew open, smashing against the wall.

"And where the fuck've you been? You been at that fuckin' kids house again? 'Cause if you have, I'll fuckin' lock yer in the shed all week again."

"No! I…I haven't. I…I was with a friend from school. Gayle. We—"

But Jean wasn't buying it. She stormed over and grabbed Claire by the arm, yanking her off the bed. Claire screamed, her mother's long nails digging into her skin. She yanked her so forcefully that her momentum caused her to stumble and collide with the wall, banging her forehead.

"The fuck do I have to do to make you listen, huh? You useless, stupid, fucked up piece of shit. Shoulda fuckin' drowned yer when yer was born. I told yer dad I was gonna do it and fuckin shoulda. His fault I didn't. A wimp and a coward, like all men."

"Mum! Please, you're hurting me. I haven't been to the neighbour's house. I swear!"

"Bullshit."

Jean slapped Claire hard across the face, making Claire's vision go blurry. Jean threw her along the landing.

"The fuck did I have to have a kid? You've been goin' to the neighbour's and blabbin', I bet. Tellin' 'em what a useless mother I am, ain't yer. Gonna get social services knockin' on my door threatenin' me, is that it?"

Jean picked up Claire by the hair and slapped her again in the face, causing Claire to howl in terror and pain.

"Mum, please stop!"

"You're sleepin' in the shed again. You can stay there all night without supper, think about what you're sayin' at school and to the neighbours. Fuckin' little bitch."

She dragged Claire to her feet and pushed her towards the stairs. But the inertia caused something to happen Jean may not have planned on. The girl fell down the stairs.

She landed at the bottom and cracked her head on the floor. Blood began to pool around her as she lay there semi-conscious.

"Fuck! Now look what you've done!"

She headed down the stairs cursing, continuing to insult her daughter, complaining about the blood staining the carpet. She prodded Claire with her foot as though she was a sleeping dog.

"You dead? You better not be. I ain't goin' to prison 'cause of you."

Claire groaned.

"Good."

Jean squatted and rolled Claire onto her back. Her face was smeared in blood, a large gash on her forehead.

"Great, fuckin' typical. Teachers see that at school, I'm definitely gettin' social services on my case. Kenny!" she yelled. "Kenny, get yer fat arse up, yer daughter fell down the stairs and needs to go to the hospital."

There was a series of grunts and moans from the living room, and Kenny came into view half asleep.

"Now what the fuck's wrong?"

"Can't yer see? She fell down the stairs, cut her head open. Get her to hospital for stitches. She might have concussion too. Last thing we need are the fuckin' social services harrassin' us."

"For fuck's sake. Never a moment's fucking peace around here."

Kenny picked her up like she was a sack of corn for the pigs and slung her over his shoulder, the blood from her face and t-shirt smearing his shirt.

Kenny returned three hours later. Claire had required seven stitches to her forehead and had severe concussion, meaning she had to stay overnight. The doctors were worried her brain had been bruised in the fall, possibly a shard of her cracked skull piercing it. It was this defining moment that psychiatrists would argue over years later.

Chapter 11

Claire ended up staying in the hospital for three days. The doctors ran multiple tests and an MRI scan but found no immediate damage to the brain, and finally she was allowed to go home. Repeatedly, the doctor in charge asked her if everything was okay at home, and every time Claire said it was. He asked her if she was eating okay because she seemed severely malnourished and was way below the average weight for someone her age and size. He asked her several times if she really had fallen down the stairs or perhaps mum or dad had been a little angry and had accidently pushed her. That Claire's body seemed to be covered in what looked like cigarette burns and scars and gashes everywhere also peeked his curiosity. Claire denied it. The doctor asked her lots of other questions, too, mainly, he said, because he didn't understand why her parents only came to visit for half an hour each day, not even bothering to question the doctors as to her wellbeing. They came each afternoon, sat with her for a short time, then made their excuses and left. They didn't even bother to bring her spare clothes, sweets or chocolate, nothing. But Claire shrugged it off.

On the morning of the fourth day, the doctor informed Claire's mother she could go home, and Kenny came to pick her up. It was a Friday, but the doctor had told her parents she should rest from school for a few days and at the slightest sign of dizziness to return immediately. He might as well have been talking to a dead person. From the moment Claire entered her home again, it was as if nothing had happened. Her mother was already drinking from the vodka bottle, and it wasn't even midday yet.

"Yer tell anyone what happened, you're sleeping in the shed. Don't forget it. Now fuck off and give me some peace and quiet for a change."

Claire headed upstairs. For a couple of days afterwards, she had headaches which the doctors had only been allowed to give mild painkillers for given her age, and she had been dizzy when she got out of bed to go to the toilet, but now she felt fine. She couldn't remember a lot about what happened anyway, only that her mother had grabbed her by the hair, and the next thing she knew she was in hospital. But she could easily guess what happened. Her mother had thrown her down the stairs in her drunken fit and nearly killed her. She had done many other terrible, cruel things to Claire, but never to the point her life was threatened. She thought she should be terrified, worried sick every time her mother got drunk and was in a bad mood, but she felt strangely calm about the whole situation. It was like she was beyond feeling scared anymore. She lay on her bed, stared up at the ceiling, and completely ignored her parents shouting and arguing downstairs.

The next morning, she woke up with the full intention of going to Michael's, telling her mother she was going for a walk as it was such a nice day for a change. Or maybe even just going anyway unannounced in case she forbid her leave the grounds. It was unlikely because her mother seemed to appreciate not having Claire around all day, but she never got the chance to leave anyway. She was heading towards the dirt track when she heard her father and others laughing and joking.

Claire stopped to see what was so funny. Her father only ever laughed when he was outside with his friends, drinking beer. She suspected he hated being at home as much as she did. Outside, he was a totally different person. He was holding a squawking, flapping chicken in the air upside-down by its legs. Whenever an animal or bird was chosen to be slaughtered, neither of her parents ever warned or told her what was going to happen, but she knew, anyway, and so would run back inside to avoid seeing it. But this time she wanted to watch.

Two friends were with her father, all three holding beer cans. There was a large gas canister beside them heating a pot of water. Her father finished his beer, threw the empty can on the ground, then placed the chicken on an old log stained with dried blood. He bent down, picked up a long knife, and in one swoop cut off the chicken's head. At that moment, he saw Claire watching them.

"Hey, Claire, come over here, it won't bite yer. Here, watch this."

He dropped the chicken on the ground and Claire watched both fascinated and shocked as the headless chicken began to run in circles, its wings flapping incessantly before it hit the ground, blood spurting from its neck and its body flipping and jerking. The three men laughed at Claire's reaction.

"You never seen that before?" asked one of them.

She shook her head.

"Well, you've heard the phrase 'running around like a headless chicken,' right?"

She shook her head again. Claire had never heard anything remotely similar.

"Well, that's what they do. Nerves and stuff." He picked up the lifeless body of the bird and held it up. "Dead now, though, see?"

Claire approached, curious, wanting to know if it really was dead or not. She couldn't understand how cutting the head off something allowed it to remain alive for so long afterwards. It made her wonder if the thing could still see too. She found that fascinating. Her father took the bird off his friend and dangled it in front of Claire's face. Drops of blood sprayed his shirt, which didn't seem to bother him at all. Then he dropped the chicken into the boiling water, and within five minutes the chicken's feathers were removed. Then he sliced open its chest, revealing still-glistening intestines. Claire peered in closer.

"Pull its guts out," said her father. "Go on, don't be a chicken."

His friends sniggered.

"That's gross, I don't want to."

"You gotta learn someday, girl. I ain't gonna be around forever, and yer mother ain't gonna do it. You're getting to be a big girl now, in more ways than one."

He stuck a hand inside the chicken's stomach, rubbed it about for a bit, then pulled it out and smeared blood over Claire's face.

"There, see, you better get used to it. You'll be dripping blood in other places soon too. And no doubt gettin' more than just blood on yer face. Then you'll be all grown up, and you can help yer father in other ways."

Claire had no idea what he was talking about, and his two friends looked a little shocked also.

Disgusted by what her father had just done, she ran to the lake and washed the blood off while he laughed at her.

She couldn't go to Michael's looking like this. She had spots of blood on her jacket as well. They'd think something was wrong and might want to bring her back here and question Claire's mother. And that couldn't happen. Instead, she went and sat under a tree in a field across the road and thought about what she'd just witnessed. She couldn't get the sight of that chicken out of her head, still apparently alive missing its head. It was impossible, it had to be. When someone's head got cut off, surely they died instantly. All animals and creatures did. Maybe chickens were special in some way. Then she had an idea and decided to go looking for any bird's nests hidden among the bushes.

***

"And that's when you decapitated the birds?"

"Yeah. Like I said, curiosity."

"Did it occur to you to try with other things too?"

"Oh yeah, obviously. There's a few stray cats that used to roam about the farm. I wanted to cut their heads off as well, but I could never catch one. I tried, leaving bits of food and stuff, but they were always too fast."

"Anything else?"

"That was when I started thinking about people. I used to fantasise about the bullies at school. Holding one down and cutting his head off, see what happened. Like, maybe he'd start flapping and jerking, too, or his eyes would blink. That use to make me shiver and giggle, imagining this kid with his head just sitting there and he's blinking and trying to talk. Can you imagine! I even thought about cutting my mother's head off while she slept at night, but then my father might wake up and phone the police, and I'd go to prison.

"Now, of course, I wish I'd gone through with it. Both their fucking heads."

"So, after you fell down the stairs, you started to feel different. Think different."

"Yeah, it was like I wasn't really scared anymore of my mother. Or the bullies. Like my emotions had suddenly been switched off. I dunno, like a zombie, oblivious to everything, except one thing."

"And what was that?"

"That people were gonna stop hurting me once and for all."

Chapter 12

Claire made sure there was no blood or feathers on her before she knocked on Michael's door. She felt no remorse for killing the baby birds, only mild disappointment that they hadn't started running around like the chicken. She wanted to know if the birds could still see, as well, after snapping their necks, but apparently not. Not that they showed any signs of doing so anyway. She decided maybe they had been too young and vowed to try and catch a bigger bird next time. Maybe steal one of her father's ducks and try it with that. Or maybe even an animal of some kind. Her father had a small pen with several rabbits in it. A rabbit would be easier to catch and wouldn't bite or snap at her as she sawed its head off. If her father noticed a rabbit missing, she could lie and say she saw a fox prowling about. Foxes were often seen hunting in the area or drinking from the lake; he wouldn't know the truth. The idea made her smile. It would be fun chopping the rabbit's head off to see what it did. Maybe it might jump about in circles for a while before collapsing. She decided she was going to find out tomorrow.

Her smile became a frown when no one came to the door. The Jeep was gone, but that might mean only Michael's dad had gone out. It was Saturday afternoon, and she was bored. Michael's parents might even treat her to McDonald's later, or take them both to a park or the cinema, especially when she told them about being in hospital. Claire had never been to the cinema and was tremendously envious of the kids at school who got to see all the good films when they came out. She couldn't imagine how exciting it must be to sit in front of such a massive screen, try popcorn for the first time, which everyone said was the best ever.

She knocked for the fifth time, banging on the door with her fists. How dare they all go out and leave her behind? They were always telling her what a good, nice girl she was and could come any time, the incident with asking Michael about sex apparently forgotten. This wasn't fair. Maybe they had been lying to her. It was all a ploy to stop her from coming here again. Well, that wasn't going to happen either. This was her home, her real family. She had already decided that when she was ten years old, and thus an adult, she was going to move in permanently and not tell her other parents anything. They wouldn't care anyway.

When no one came still she kicked the door, swore, and fuming, headed back home. She was so angry that if she stumbled upon a bird or animal of any kind she would have torn its head off with her bare hands. Not wanting to go home even though she was hungry, she spent the afternoon hunting any injured birds or animals along the hedges in the field opposite. She imagined catching a rabbit or hare or baby deer and squeezing its neck until the head popped off, then laughing hysterically as the creature ran around in circles, its eyes following her before dying. She also imagined squeezing Michael's or his parents' throats, too, for abandoning her again. When she did arrive home and heard her parents fighting and screaming, a bottle smashing against a wall, she went to bed hungry. The cupboards were empty anyway.

As usual, her parents slept in later Sundays, so she was up and on her way to Michael's before they even awoke. She found some stale bread in the cupboard, something resembling meat hidden at the back of the fridge, and made a sandwich, scoffing it down as though starving. Which she was. This time when she arrived at Michael's cottage, the Jeep was there. It had been a while since she last saw Michael or his parents, and it felt like a month had passed. Claire was excited to see them again. She would stay and have a hot roast dinner with them. They'd shower her with ice cream and cake afterwards, apologising profusely for not being around for her. They would take her to the cinema then McDonald's after. She knocked on the door, a big smile on her face in anticipation of having a fun day for once. It was Martin who answered.

"Hey there, Claire. You're up early today. Everything okay?"

"Yeah. I missed you all. I came yesterday but no one was home."

There came the sound of crying from the living room, which made Claire apprehensive. Had she been wrong after all and the same happened here as it did at her own home?

"Ah, yeah. Well, we've been out for most of the time. At least me and Michael have, his mother all the time. We have a new member of the family. Wanna come see?"

Claire nodded and smiled, but inside a knot was twisting itself in her stomach. Martin led her to the living room, where Michael and Kathleen were cuddled together, big, stupid smiles on their faces as Kathleen rocked the crying baby back and forth.

"Hi, Claire! Meet Tania," said Kathleen.

Michael barely glanced at her. Martin went and sat next to his wife, stroking the baby, all three completely ignoring Claire, as though she wasn't even present. Almost a full minute later, when they still hadn't so much as glanced at Claire, she tried to squeeze in beside them on the sofa.

"Careful, Claire. Give her some room to breathe," said Martin, practically pushing her off. They continued making cooing noises and chuckling among themselves.

"Wanna go play on the PlayStation, Michael?"

He shook his head, not even bothering to look at her.

"I came by yesterday, but no one was home. Now I know why. I was really bored at home. I had to go to hospital too. I fell down the stairs and had to have loads of stitches. Look."

Martin and Kathleen looked up at Claire's face and both frowned.

"How did you do that, Claire? That must have been really painful and scary," said Kathleen.

"It was. I fell and the doctor said I was…un…un…I was knocked out for a while, and I had to stay in hospital for three days. I still get dizzy and have to take lots of pills, and the doctor said I was lucky to live. It really hurt, and I was so scared, and there was loads of blood, and…"

But while they might have been listening, they weren't even looking. She thought she had their full attention and they would stop fussing over the baby and fuss over her instead, but it wasn't happening. Her intestines felt like someone was twisting them or had set them on fire. She looked down to see her hands were clenched into fists.

"Well, that's terrible, Claire. You should be more careful, you know. Michael, you wanna go get a nappy for me? I think your sister has had an accident."

All three chuckled.

Claire wanted to cry. This wasn't how it was supposed to play out at all. They should have been in utter shock and smothering Claire with hugs and kisses, telling her how brave she was and how sorry they were, and all four of them were to go immediately to the toy shop and buy her a present. That she was to stay and live with them now; with them as her parents, they wouldn't let something like that ever happen, but as usual in Claire's life, it was as if she was missing, a ghost always hovering in the background, unseen and unwanted. It seemed there was always something or someone more important than her, ready to steal from her what she craved the most—love and attention. Her moist eyes focused on the baby.

"Can I hold her?"

"No, I think not, Claire. Not yet. Maybe when she's a bit older. We wouldn't want you to drop her, would we!"

Michael returned with a nappy and handed it to his mother. Kathleen went to work changing the nappy while they made exaggerated shows of Tania's nappy smelling bad.

"Oww, my head really hurts again. But I don't wanna go back to the hospital. I'm scared what they might do. And...and my mum and dad don't even bother coming to see me, and I don't wanna be alone, and..."

She rubbed the scar across her forehead, swaying on her feet, forcing tears to run down her face.

"Aww, maybe you should go home, Claire, and tell your mother. You shouldn't be out if you still feel unwell. It's getting late, anyway, and we have friends and family coming over soon. Martin, why don't you drive Claire home quickly?"

Martin frowned. Only a second, but Claire caught it. That frown symbolised everything that was happening in her life right now. And she hated it all. She glared at Tania and wondered if she would flap around on the floor, too, if she cut her head off.

Chapter 13

For a while, Claire had considered going to school. Maybe this time, with the scar on her forehead still clearly visible, the kids might take pity on her for a change. And when she told them she'd fallen down the stairs and had been unconscious and in hospital for three days, they might even be in awe. They might tell her how brave she was, not just call her a smelly, stupid farm girl, but she would be someone to be *admired*. They might crowd around her and ask her what it was like to be unconscious, if it was like being dead then coming back to life again, and she would exaggerate and tell them that yes, it had been like dying. But she hadn't cried, not even when she was lying in a massive pool of her own blood and her parents had screamed. But not her. No, she had been very brave and hadn't even flinched when the stitches were put in. She might be their new best friend forever. And if they laughed at her, well, maybe she would find a way of slapping that smile from their faces. At some point over the last few days, she had decided she'd had enough of being laughed at and insulted. It might just be time to put an end to all that, sooner rather than later.

But her mother ruined any hopes of becoming a hero for her.

"I wish yer could go to school, but yer can't. Teachers find out you're there when you ain't supposed to, they might send social services over, and I ain't havin' that. So you'll have to wait. Stay in yer room or somethin', or go fuck off outside, just make sure yer keep outta my way. I got a headache."

Claire thought of arguing her case. The idea of hanging about alone all day was not a pleasant one. And she was still fuming over being rejected by Michael's parents yesterday, traded for the new member of the family when she was supposed to be that person. *Maybe I should go there today*, she wondered, *while Michael is at school? Perhaps if it's just me and that stupid baby they might pay me more attention. Take me to the park or something and then McDonald's afterwards.* Yes, this was a very good idea. While she waited for them to get ready, she could play on Michael's computer, maybe delete his games on purpose for ignoring her yesterday.

Her decision made, she dressed in the same clothes as the day before, not bothering to brush her greasy, unwashed hair, and headed outside. But she stopped when she saw the small crowd gathered near the pig pens. Her dad was there with his friends and others she didn't recognise, both men and women. They were all laughing and joking, but she wasn't sure why. A woman was wearing a plastic apron and holding a large bucket. Even more ominous was her father holding a large knife in one hand and a massive wooden mallet in the other. He put them down to one side and started chatting with the strangers. Claire was surprised to see them hand money to him, which he quickly put in his back pocket. Curious, Claire approached closer and watched behind a large oak tree near the lake.

The pigs were all grunting and snorting, standing on their hind legs and watching over the top of the wall, as if curious too. Her dad kept pointing to the one nearest, in the first pen, a massive, bloated sow with bloodshot eyes, its tail flicking constantly. Once

Kenny had collected the money from them all, he picked up a length of rope that had a small loop at the end and entered the pig's enclosed area.

"This is gonna be amazing!" said one woman. "I always wondered how they made it, now we'll get to see."

"Nothing better than eating something you prepared yourself. Makes it taste better, I always say. My grandmother insisted that the chickens she had in her yard always tasted better than those bought from the supermarket," replied a man next to her.

"It'll be fun!" said another woman.

After more discussion on the preparation of certain foods, her father grabbed the rope and opened the first pen. The pig's back foot stepped onto the loop, and her father tugged, closing it. He gave the length of rope to his friend, and the small crowd parted as the pig lazily left the pen into open ground. Claire watched, mesmerised.

She jumped and gasped as her dad brought up the mallet over his shoulder and brought it down hard on the pig's skull, a resounding thud echoing around the farm. The pig crumpled instantly and spasmed violently.

"Hold on tight now, don't let go, and watch out for it kicking. If it gets you in the ribs, it'll break 'em."

His friends quickly grabbed onto a hoof each with both hands, visibly struggling to contain the pig's dying spasms, while he picked up the knife and slashed open its throat. The woman wearing the apron put the bucket under the pig's throat as the blood poured, rapidly filling the bucket. The other pigs must have sensed what was happening because they became agitated, grunting louder and faster, hopping from one foot to the other as if trying to offer encouragement to their dying friend. Claire, her jaw dropped yet smiling, as though seeing something utterly wonderful for the first time, watched as the woman stuck her hand in the bucket and began to swirl the blood around, splashing her apron and even her face, completely oblivious to it covering her skin. From her position, Claire could smell the rich, coppery aroma of fresh blood, and it was a smell that would follow her forever, like a terrible secret.

The flow of blood seemed endless. The woman continued swirling, the thick liquid now up to her elbow, most of her face and chest covered in it. The onlookers looked just as amazed, big grins on their faces. Claire thought of the birds she'd killed and the chicken flapping around. The almost-dead pig was looking straight at her, as though pleading for help, and so she waved at it, hoping it might suddenly jump up and start racing around madly, its head lolling from side to side, up and down, almost completely severed from the rest of its body. But to Claire's disappointment, none of that happened. The pig gave one last violent spasm and died. Some of the onlookers clapped, occasionally patting the woman with the apron on the back as though congratulating her. This scene was also something Claire would never forget and would relive time and time again.

She had been a little scared seeing how violently the pig lashed out, its enormous, bloated body flapping like a fish, but now that it was dead, she felt compelled to get even closer. She wanted to see inside the pig, how it was made. Just as she had experimented with the baby birds, lots of ideas floated through her mind of what she'd like to do to the pig. She wanted to grab the knife from her dad's hand and embed it deep into the pig's belly, see what came out, touch whatever came out. Unfortunately, this time at least, she didn't get the chance. The pig now dead, her dad and his friends struggled to pick up the animal and lay it on a table after the last of the blood had drained from its neck. The woman picked up her bucket and headed off to a large shed. The others turned the pig onto its back, and her dad easily slit the pig's belly open, its intestines spilling out like trapped animals. He began hacking and slicing and dropped the severed guts into another bucket, loud, wet, squelching sounds as they landed. The onlookers pointed at the various intestines and organs, debating among themselves which was which. They were all smiling as they did so. Claire would later learn they had actually paid her father just so they could watch the pig being slaughtered and turned into various types of meat. It was something she would reflect upon later, after she heard her father telling his friends how much he earned from such an event.

She heard words spoken among them as her father explained what each cut would be used for. They sounded like foreign words. Things like *chorizo, morcilla, jamón*. She recognised sausage easy enough though. Once he'd disembowelled the pig, he took a small axe and chopped off each leg, the tail, and finally the head. His friends helped him carry the various parts to the shed. Claire hurried over to the carcass as soon as they'd gone, unable to stop herself.

The smell of it was atrocious, but this didn't bother her. Flies were already settling on the body in swarms, delighted with their newfound abode, and this didn't bother her either. She was too immersed in the experience to worry about that. This was the first time ever she had seen a large animal dead, its insides scooped out. She touched the thick layers of fat and was surprised to find they were warm. When she pushed hard enough up through the throat, her hand came out the other end, wet and sticky. This made her giggle, seeing her hand there instead of the pig's head.

"Hello, Mr Piggy!" she said, wiggling her fingers.

She pulled her hand out, sticky and covered in blood and some fatty substance. She dared to lick a finger, not quite sure why, and didn't recoil at the taste. Another desire overcame her—to crawl into the carcass as though crawling into a sleeping bag. It would make a super cool hiding place if Gayle or Michael ever came over and they played hide and seek. Perhaps her dad could fashion some kind of zip on its stomach. But more than that, she wanted to imagine how it must feel to be eaten by some giant monster, slowly being digested by its acids, trapped forever, and the only escape would be via its bowels. Imagine it was Michael trapped in there, screaming to be freed; it could be his punishment for completely ignoring her the other day. Or maybe the baby. Even better. She was the cause for Claire's sudden loneliness once again. But above all, what Claire wanted and fantasised about was taking that knife from her father, slitting Michael's and his family's throats, then do as the woman with the apron did— let their blood flood the big bucket while she swirled it around, happily playing like a toddler splashing about in a kiddie pool.

She was about to climb up onto the table and climb inside the carcass when she heard voices—her dad and the small crowd were returning. Claire ran to her original hiding place and watched as the rest of the pig was deftly cut up, the pieces wrapped up and shared among the crowd like trophies. She heard her dad telling them that when the morcilla and other meats were ready he'd send them out to them all too. They thanked him effusively and left. That night, Claire dreamed she was a pig walking around with her dad's big butcher knife and opening up the stomachs of every single person that had ever hurt or abandoned her. It was a long dream.

Chapter 14

The next day, still not allowed to go to school, Claire spent most of the morning in her bedroom alone. She could hear her mother downstairs cursing and swearing because she was almost out of cigarettes. She heard her mother stomp upstairs, muttering to herself about how hard life was and she was tired and no one ever fucking helped out in this house, she had to do everything herself. Claire listened, not caring anymore. Only a few days ago she would have been huddled against the wall praying her mother didn't take out her rage on her. It seemed she liked taking out her frustrations on Claire, using any excuse to slap or punch her or lock her in the dreaded shed with the spiders and bugs, often naked or in her thin pyjamas so she spent the whole night shivering and pacing back and forth to try and keep warm. Sometimes she would get terrible aches in her sides from shivering so violently, begging and screaming to be let out. But since falling down the stairs, her mother had barely put a hand on her. She had even ensured Claire ate properly twice a day. She would complain about it to her father, something about social services coming at any moment. Claire didn't know what the social services were, but it sounded frightening. Enough to worry her mother anyway.

Jean came out of her room, stomped down the stairs, and then there was a loud bang as the front door slammed shut. She must have gone into the village to buy cigarettes, Claire figured. This was good, too, because Claire had noticed that when her mother didn't have cigarettes, she was often in an even fouler mood than usual.

Thinking about that, she decided that later, when school was over, she'd go back to Michael's and stay for a while. Maybe they were bored with the baby now and would play with her again like before. She spent the rest of the day wandering around the adjacent fields, looking for any injured birds or animals she could catch. She also had a knife with her she'd taken from the kitchen. Not only was she obsessed with Michael and his parents ignoring her, she was also obsessed over what she witnessed with the pig yesterday. She wanted to see other animal's insides too.

Claire was a little downhearted when she knocked on Michael's door that afternoon. She hadn't found a single thing she could cut up and dissect. She'd been really excited about that, too, so instead she hid the knife in Michael's garden and waited for him to answer. She knew they were home because their cars were parked outside and there was a light on upstairs. She knocked again, hoping they would invite her to stay for dinner. A burger and chips would be amazing, she told herself, with heaps of ketchup poured onto it. Yesterday, her mother had allowed Claire to put ketchup on her sausage for once, and she had instantly associated it with all the blood being swirled around in the bucket while the pig was being slaughtered. She poured as much ketchup as she was allowed and drowned her sausage in it. Every time Claire saw something red, her mind invariably went back to that moment. And she saw red everywhere.

A knot began to form in her stomach. She

knocked again, louder and longer, practically pummelling the door. She peered through the keyhole looking for signs of movement, perhaps the baby crying, but all was silent and still. They were home, she knew perfectly well. Michael's mother often complained when he left the lights on, saying it cost money, and there was a light on in Michael's bedroom. Yet when she stepped back and looked up, it had been switched off. Then she saw the slightest twitch of the curtain, as though someone had been peering out from the tightest of corners.

Her lips twitched, too, as her jaw tightened and she ground her teeth together. Her nerves were alive, causing a rush of adrenaline to course through her, heart pumping furiously. Her muscles tensed like rocks, head throbbing with fury. For the briefest of moments, she considered grabbing the knife, barging into the house, and searching for Michael. She'd bury the blade into his throat, watch the blood cascade like the blood from the pig's throat. Claire looked down at her hands to see they were clenched into tight fists, imprints left by her fingernails on her palms. She used her fists to bang on the door, kicking it too. The door shuddered in the old frame.

"I know you're there! You let me in!" she screamed as she stepped back again and looked up. This time Michael had been too slow. He had been peering out from the curtain once more, holding that stupid baby. He jumped back just as she looked up. She searched for a stone to throw at his window, but the garden was well kept, the grass neatly cut, and she found nothing. She thought she caught a glimpse of movement in the living room, too, when she glanced that way, but nothing moved now. His parents were surely ignoring her as well, not wanting her inside their home anymore. They were all in it together. Claire had been replaced by a stupid, crying baby.

She thought of kicking the door again, but her body was aching from being tense for so long. They weren't going to let her in, that much was clear. She considered once more just barging in and hunting them down but decided against it. It was okay, no problem. She'd deal with Michael in good time. Perhaps she would make him squeal and grunt like the pig had done. Claire retrieved her knife and headed back to the farm.

As she entered the grounds, she saw her mother walking off towards the house with one of the fishermen. He had a hand on her behind, squeezing her buttocks. Claire watched in disgust as she returned the compliment by squeezing him between the legs. Her father was nowhere to be seen so was either down at the local pub with friends or inside taking a nap.

All the while she walked home, she had been thinking about how much she'd like to hurt Michael. He had hurt her for the second time in a week. It was as if they didn't care at all she had been in hospital for three days after almost killing herself. Totally irrelevant as far as they were concerned. Like she was an ant, a bug, something that might never have existed, and if it did, it went completely undetected. She was tired of being hurt all the time and concluded it was time others saw and felt the suffering she went through. Michael and his parents were going to be sorry for shutting her out like that.

The desire to cry had disappeared days ago. Rage

and anger were her principal companions now. A duck flapped and quacked nearby, making her jump. Slowly, she headed over to it, the birds used to human presence. When she was next to it, just before it returned to the pond, she squatted and quickly grabbed it around the neck. It flapped and croaked, startled and frightened. Claire took it to the table where the pig had been slaughtered. Changing its throat for its feet, she held it down tight, brought out the knife, and stabbed the bird in the neck. Its flapping and squawking intensified, but she held it down firmly and proceeded to saw its head off. Once done, she threw the bird to the ground to see if it acted like the chicken. Disappointed that it didn't and was already dead, she picked it back up again and stabbed it multiple times, everywhere she could, until her arm ached. Then she slit its stomach open and with her bare hand pulled out its intestines and organs until nothing more than an empty carcass remained. She was panting by now, but still furious, continuing to stab at the organs, the body, slashing and tearing until it was reduced to small pieces. She was covered in blood and feathers, bits of intestines stuck to her coat. As a final act, she picked up the head and scooped out the eyes, throwing them at the other ducks like marbles. Then she stabbed its head until its brain leaked through the gashes, dripping down the table with the other secretions. It was only when she finally stopped, nothing left to stab anymore, that she realised she had been yelling Michael's name with every thrust of the blade into the dead bird. Disgusted, she threw the remains into the pond and headed home. She was starving hungry and was going to demand something hot with lots and lots of ketchup on it to eat.

Chapter 15

Saturday came, a day Claire had been waiting for. This time there would be no reason for Michael not to be at home unless his parents had decided on a family day out. Spoiled brat. For Claire, the idea of a day out meant being dragged to the supermarket to do the weekly shopping, told to keep her mouth shut and not ask for anything because she wasn't getting it anyway. For her, it was a form of psychological torture. Seeing all the other kids, or at least the majority, begging and pleading for their favourite breakfast cereals or sweets and biscuits, big, silly smiles glued to their faces as their wishes were granted. Sometimes, as if there was some secret conspiracy between them all, they would look at Claire with their gleaming smiles and bright, wide eyes as if they could read her thoughts. *I bet you wish you could have this, too, don't you? But you can't. It's all mine and no one else's. And I'm gonna eat it all until I puke.* Normally, it was her father who did the weekly shopping because her mother was too busy and didn't like crowds, she said, and sometimes, after her father had been to her room the night before, he would allow her a chocolate bar. Only one, of course, and it had to be eaten before they got home or her mother would call her a fat, demanding pig, and as punishment that little chocolate bar was going to be her supper as well. But those times, Claire didn't care. It was worth it just to enjoy the measly bar, trying to make it last as long as possible.

But today, her mother had to go into the village

and didn't want Claire coming with her. Which was fine. Claire had already made her plans. She was going to be at Michael's house before they had time to go out themselves. As soon as she finished her breakfast—cereals mixed with water instead of milk because milk was so expensive these days—she left before her mother could ask her where she was going. Not that she cared anyway.

As she expected, both their cars were parked outside when she arrived at Michael's cottage. She had full intentions of staying here all day, whether they liked it or not. If they were indeed planning a day out, she was going with them. Any attempt of telling her that no, she couldn't go, she had already planned for such an event. No one was going to tell her no anymore. She'd fake a dizzy spell, sob her heart out that no, she didn't want to go home anymore because her mother did bad things to her and her father made her feel uncomfortable lots of times, especially at night when mum was asleep and he came into her room and touched her. She would say he made her touch his *thing* and do other things, and that mum beat and starved her, liked to lock her in the shed in only her pyjamas. That when she was drunk and Claire had misbehaved in some way, she would drag Claire to the duck pond in the middle of the night while wearing only her pyjamas and throw her in, not letting her out of the freezing water until fifteen minutes had passed. That one night she made Claire lick some of the duck shit splattered around the pond, and if she puked it back up again, she would be made to eat that too. Claire would tell them all this, and they would be horrified and insist Claire stayed and lived with them from now on.

She was just about to walk down the garden path when the front door opened. No entirely sure why, she ducked behind the wall and hurried around the corner so they wouldn't see her. She heard Michael's and his father's voices. They were joking about something, both laughing. Claire considered showing herself, but then she heard what they were joking about and it made Claire furious.

"Well, I have to be honest," said Martin, "she is a bit weird. Living on a farm, I guess. And yeah, you're right, she does smell a bit like pig poo. But don't you dare tell her I said that or you're not getting the new Nikes next week!"

Michael burst out laughing, then made oinking noises. "I bet she sleeps with them like they're her pets or something. Maybe she has a pig sleep in her bed at night instead of a cat or dog!"

"Michael, don't be nasty. Poor girl. She can't help it if she's brought up on a farm. I don't think she's a good influence around here, anyway, especially with your baby sister about. If she comes back again, I think I'll tell her she's not welcome anymore. She makes me nervous the way she looked at the baby the other day. Like she's jealous or something. So, if she does come back, you do like I said the other day: don't answer the door. And if she starts kicking it and screaming again like last week, I'll drag her back home and tell her mother."

"Good. I never liked her much anyway."

The car doors opened, the engine started up, and they drove off. Claire's immediate reaction was to slide down the wall and burst out crying, holding her head in her hands. Everyone hated her. Everyone laughed at her behind her back. She could die right now and no one would care at all. Like the pig the other day, people might even pay to come and watch her being chopped up, made into sausages, her blood swirled about in a bucket. And they would cheer and clap and joke about how stupid she was and smelled like one of those fucking pigs.

Claire stopped crying. Despair was gone now, replaced by rage and a need for revenge. She had already learned crying wasn't getting her anywhere because no one gave a shit about her. They would soon, though. Once the car was out of sight, she stood up and headed down the garden path. She considered knocking then decided against it, peering through the letterbox instead. All was silent in the house. She tried the door. It opened, so she stepped inside, keeping as quiet as possible, straining to hear any noise. If Kathleen caught her, she would say the door was opened and she was worried about burglars. Claire headed to the living room, peered in, and saw it was empty; she did the same in the kitchen. Kathleen was upstairs, then, probably asleep still. Even better.

Claire tiptoed up the stairs and dared to poke her head in Kathleen's bedroom, the door slightly ajar. She had expected to see the baby in bed with her, but there was no cot and Kathleen was sprawled out in bed alone, snoring softly. She stared at her for a moment, wondering if she had said the same things about Claire, too, joking that Claire was weird and smelly and wasn't to come here anymore. She thought she probably did. Her heart was thudding rapidly in her chest, and not just from the buzz she was feeling from being in their home uninvited. It was also because she was trying to imagine what it would feel like to take a great butcher's knife and sink it into Kathleen's stomach, opening her up and pulling out all her intestines. She imagined all Kathleen's blood pouring into a large pot, and Claire would swirl it about, getting covered in it herself. Then she would take it downstairs and boil it, having first learned how to make the black sausage it was to be used for, then feed it to Michael and his dad. That would be funny.

She imagined cutting off Kathleen's head and the woman running around in circles, flapping her arms before collapsing, and this was very funny. Claire had to slap a hand over her mouth to stifle a giggle. Before she made a mistake and accidently woke her, Claire left the room and headed next door to the baby's room. As Claire approached the sleeping girl, she noticed a baby monitor beside the cot. She turned it off, and as with Kathleen, she stood staring at the tiny creature. It was all her fault, and she didn't even know it yet. She was completely innocent right now, but like everyone else she would probably grow up to be horrible and nasty. A monster. A pig. She had come into this world to replace Claire, a stupid little thing that was more important than she was now, and it wasn't fair. *How could a stupid little baby be more important than me?* she wondered. She was only a few weeks old, and her room had more dolls and stuffed teddy bears than Claire had ever had in her entire life. There was a small, stuffed animal beside the baby, a cat. Claire picked it up and pulled its head off, then pulled out all the stuffing inside. She went around the room and did the same to all the others she could find, throwing the white stuffing into the air so it looked like it was snowing. This helped to release some of the rage inside her, but it wasn't enough. Conscious that Kathleen could wake up at any second, she very gently picked up the baby and carried her downstairs.

The baby could wake at any second and start crying, so she laid her down on the kitchen table as gently as possible then stepped back. In a way, she thought it looked like a pig, all fat and wrinkly, pink skin, no hair on its body. It was disgusting, a freak. This was a freak, not Claire. She spat on its chest then thrust a finger up her nose and wiped what she pulled out over its body too. If she had the time, she would have squatted over it and peed on it, but she didn't have time unfortunately. So, she turned her attention to what was around her.

After rooting around for a while, she found it–the large meat cleaver. She picked it up. It was heavy and looked very sharp. Claire turned back to the baby and stood there watching it again, an intense hate towards it that represented all the bad and horrible things that were happening to her in her life. The baby opened its eyes, staring at Claire as if challenging her. A couple of seconds later the first wail erupted from its mouth. It was its only wail.

Claire brought down the cleaver as hard as she could on its throat.

Its pathetic wailing was abruptly cut short as a spray of blood shot into the air, soaking the table and getting on Claire's face and coat. She had to use both hands to pull out the cleaver, wiggling it side to side to free it. She raised the cleaver above her head and brought it down a second time. The head was easily separated from the rest of the body. Claire watched in awe and amazement, unable to believe something so small could contain this amount of blood. The table was already soaked in it, and still more came from the open neck. She smiled.

"Oink, oink," she whispered. "Who's the piggy now? You are."

She picked up the head and brought it close to her face then jabbed a finger into its eyeballs, pressing down hard to see what happened. They were like jelly and popped from their sockets, dangling there like yo-yo's. Claire pulled them off and threw them at the wall, where they first stuck there then slowly slid down, leaving behind slimy trails like she'd seen snails do. But she wasn't finished yet.

She picked it up by its feet and let it sway back and forth, blood still dripping from the wound. Then she swung it around the kitchen so the walls were splashed in it too. As the last of the blood dripped onto the floor, she put it back on the table, picked up the cleaver, and re-enacted what her father had done, hacking its stomach open until all its tiny organs and intestines were revealed. Arms and legs were sliced off, chunks of flesh fell to the floor. A sudden bout of rage overcame her. For all the terrible things done and said to her. All the times her mother had beaten her, locked her in the shed, stubbed out cigarettes on her, pushed her down the stairs. For her father who did bad things to her when she was in bed. For the kids at school who tormented incessantly. And, most of all, for this stupid thing and its brother and parents who had pushed her away like everyone else had done. She reached into the belly and began to frantically pull and tug at the intestines and organs, not knowing which was which and not caring, and threw them around the room. Some landed and stuck to the ceiling and walls; a string of intestines wrapped itself around the swinging lightbulb like a tail. She cut off one of Tania's hands and toes and put them in the fridge. Glancing over at Tania's head, an uncontrollable urge to jump up and down on her head came over her, so that's what she did, jumping and kicking while laughing hysterically. She picked up the head and kicked it across the room. "Goal!" she yelled as it came to rest between two chair legs.

Claire was only mildly surprised to realise she was crying as she did so. And it must have been quite loud, because she could hear a noise coming from upstairs, the sound of creaking floorboards. She threw the dead creature away and quickly made her way out. She really wished she could have stayed to see Kathleen's face, but she would have to imagine it instead. And Claire had a very vivid imagination.

She was humming to herself and practically floating as she reached home, never so happy as now, proud of what she had done. She had taught them a lesson. Now they could never swap her for the stupid baby because it wasn't around anymore. *Maybe*, she thought, *if I'm really nice, they might let me play in their home again, like before.* When she stepped into her home, her mother was standing in the kitchen smoking a cigarette. She turned to face Claire and the cigarette fell from her hand, her eyes widening in disbelief.

"Hi, Mummy. Guess what I did?!"

Chapter 16

Martin wasn't entirely sure what it was he was hearing when he and Michael arrived back home from grocery shopping. As he stepped out of the car, his first thought was that Kathleen was watching some horror movie she had a soft spot for with the volume on full. This was totally out of character because it would either wake or scare Tania. When Tania was asleep, everyone had to walk around the house practically tiptoeing. The slightest noise from any of them and Kathleen would go berserk, saying the only bit of peace she got all day or night was when Tania was sleeping. So what was going on with all the screaming and howling? Michael looked up at him with concern and bewilderment in his eyes too.

It took him several seconds to fully understand what was happening because it could only mean one thing, the one thing that could not ever possibly happen. Not in his house anyway.

"Michael, stay here a moment, okay?"

Michael nodded.

Martin rushed as fast as leaden feet would allow and burst in. Now inside, the screaming sounded ten times louder, a monologue of wails and screams and Tania's name repeated over and over. He thought he already knew what had happened even though he tried to deny it; yet even so, when he ran into the kitchen, nothing could ever have prepared him for what he saw. Something that did indeed look like a horror movie set, but unfortunately it was being played in his own home. He had been about to yell his wife's name, ask her what the fuck was going on, when he froze at the entrance to the kitchen. Again, his mind playing tricks on him, refusing to accept the inevitable, for the briefest of moments, he felt a sense of relief. His and Kathleen's biggest fear, the thing neither of them discussed openly but was always present every time they went to check Tania was okay, her little chest still rising and falling, had been a false alarm. His brain told him that an accident had taken place in the kitchen, and for reasons he couldn't begin to understand, somehow Kathleen had managed to decorate the walls and floor with ketchup. This was why she had crumpled to the floor howling, because a terrible mess had been made which was going to take hours to clean up, and she was so, so tired lately already. But that thought lasted barely a second.

Still his brain refused to cooperate. It made no sense at all. Kathleen had been preparing lunch and had had an accident. She had been cutting the roast, cut herself badly, and now the roast was strewn about everywhere. There was a length of intestines still dangling from the blood-splattered lightbulb. What looked like a liver or kidney dangled from the corner of the cupboard like some obscene ornament. Another organ stuck to the fridge was slowly sliding down, leaving a glistening, sticky trail behind it. Then, his blurry eyes took in the carcass on the table, and he knew it was no turkey or chicken Kathleen had been preparing. It was quite hard to determine at first exactly what it was until his brain made the connections. Barely an inch of her pink skin was visible, barely an area that hadn't been violently slashed open exposing bone and muscle tissue.

During his training as criminal psychologist, he

had seen footage of various crime scenes and had been asked to explain the reasoning behind such savagery, what could be behind the need for the perpetrator to inflict such terrible injuries. The image that stayed with him the most was of a teenage boy that had been stabbed over fifty times. The killer's name had been Harold Saggerbob, infamous murderer of children many years ago. When he first saw the image, Martin had found it almost impossible to identify the remains as human. It looked like a fox or some other large animal had been hit by a speeding vehicle then dragged for several feet along the tarmac, its skin torn from its body in the process.

The tiny creature laying on his kitchen table resembled the teenage boy in every way except for being so tiny. An arm had almost been sliced off. A foot was only fixed to the leg by one tendon. The chest was one big, gaping, empty hole, tiny ribs jutting out like some predator baring its teeth. At the neck where the head should have been, tendrils and muscle strands fanned out like worms. And then he looked on the floor beside the table and saw his daughter's severed head looking back up at him, except there was nothing to look at him with because there only remained two, blood-filled craters where the eyeballs should have been. Her cheeks had been slashed open, showing the tiny cheekbones, nose sliced in two, and from her mouth protruded the handle of a knife, the blade embedded in the back of the throat. Her head also appeared flattened.

His legs gave way and he slumped to the floor. As he did so, his knee connected with his daughter's head, and it skated away like one of Michael's small hotwheel cars. He watched it whirl before coming to a stop, the knife still protruding like a stake, and glanced up at his wife. He couldn't say anything even if he wanted to, let alone reach out for her as she appeared to be doing to him. He couldn't even really hear her anymore; his mind had locked down in disbelief. Then Michael stepped into the kitchen, and Martin heard his scream. He also saw his son's jeans darken around the groin, a puddle appearing next to other multiple puddles on the floor, now coagulating. He didn't know how long he sat there in a frozen, zombified state. It could have been minutes or hours, yet one image did flash before him like an old memory before his body slowly began to recover from its vegetative state: that of Claire looking down at Tania with what he had only been able to comprehend as a palpable hatred towards her.

When he regained some semblance of a functioning body and mind, he slowly pulled himself to his feet and went to his wife. He tried to pull her up, too, but her legs kept giving way and she fell back down again, her bare feet slipping in a pool of blood. She had long since lost all strength and energy to scream anymore and was now whimpering, muttering something barely audible. He looked for Michael, but he had gone. It didn't even occur to him go look where he went. Martin pulled his phone from his jacket pocket, and after three attempts managed to dial the emergency services. It took several attempts from the woman on the other end to get Martin to explain what the emergency was. As though speaking through another, like a ventriloquist's dummy, he was able to mumble his baby's name, pronounce the word dead, and more or less give his address. The act of finally being able to do something constructive seemed to shake the shock from his system somewhat. His brain began to make connections. Answers to impossible questions formed, and with each one it was Claire's face that appeared. Somehow, for reasons he wouldn't be able to explain yet, and perhaps never, despite his training, this was Claire's doing. She had walked into their home and savagely and brutally mutilated an innocent baby.

The first streams of adrenaline swam up through his blood, the utter despair slowly replaced by another sensation. Right now, there was only one thing on his mind. It didn't matter that his wife and son needed him, that already he could hear the sounds of multiple sirens in the distance. The training he had undertaken for the last few years was telling him an outcome before it had even started the long and arduous process of being played out. What good was it going to do arresting a seven-year-old girl? They might as well arrest a dog as the culprit. Still unsteady, Martin left behind a scene that was going to haunt him for the rest of his life and headed towards his car. Somehow, he made it to Claire's farm without crashing into a lamp post or tree, while police cars and an ambulance raced past him heading in the opposite direction.

He walked purposefully down the path towards the front door and banged on it hard with his fist. He didn't stop banging until someone finally came and threw the door wide open.

"What the fuck you think you're do—" began who he assumed to be Claire's mother.

Martin was the classic definition of a pacificist.

He had never gotten into a fight in his life, and whenever he had been the target for anyone looking for trouble, he always managed to talk his way out of a confrontation and calm things down. The whole point of him wanting to be a criminal psychologist was so he could try to learn the reasons behind such behaviour and maybe, he often liked to fantasise, help prevent it in people before it happened. Learn to detect certain characteristics in children that were often associated as being red flags so they could be helped before their anger issues escalated. His father was a surgeon and his mother a nurse, so maybe empathy had been in his genes before he was even born, destined to help others in one way or another. He had even moved to Bradwell fifteen years ago so he could be closer to Northgate Hospital for the Criminally Insane, his idea being to perhaps interview the patients there, find out what made them so cruel and evil. Yet when he suggested it to his professor at Norwich University, it had been quickly made clear that it was impossible. Those imprisoned at Northgate were spawn from hell, he had said, monsters spat out from the darkest realms with only one idea in mind, and nothing and no one was going to help them.

Yet, with all his studying and the knowledge he had acquired, ironically enough, he had failed to spot the tell-tale signs in a little girl right in front of his very eyes. And now it was too late to do anything about it. Except for one thing. Something he had never felt in his entire life, an alien concept. A need for revenge.

"Where is she?" he croaked, his lips and mouth far too dry, the adrenaline and rage in his body making it impossible to articulate his words properly. He would have wrapped his hands around her throat had Claire herself opened the door, yet somehow he managed to suppress the desire to do so to Claire's mother.

"The fuck you talking about? Don't you come knockin' on my do—"

"Your fucking daughter! Where is she? She killed…she killed my baby! My fucking baby. She's a monster. Where is she?"

Something changed in her face. The scowl on her features momentarily dropped, her bloodshot eyes widened briefly. A look of shock and terror. It told Martin that maybe she knew exactly what he was talking about.

A shadow flitted behind the woman.

"I…I don't know what the fuck you're talking about. I'm callin' the police. Don't you come knockin' on my door spouting tha—"

"Where the fuck is she?!" he yelled. He tried to barge his way in this time, but the woman seemed to be prepared for such an eventuality and stood firm. The shadow revealed itself, clutching her mother's skirt and peering from behind. She was smiling.

"Hello, Mr Forsyth," she said. "Can I come over and play today?"

But before Martin could force his way in and strangle the girl, his arm was gripped forcefully, and two police officers pulled him back.

Chapter 17

Claire's parents fidgeted nervously across the interview room from her. Both stared at the floor, fiddling with their hands. For the second time in her life, she saw fear in their eyes. Fear, confusion, and worry. When she had arrived home and her mother had seen her covered in blood, she first thought Claire had killed one of the animals, a pig given the amount of blood on her, and her arm was already swung back ready to hit her until Claire told her the truth. It had taken three attempts for Jean to light a cigarette as she processed the news. Then, unexpectedly, instead of phoning the police or punishing her in some way as she usually would, Jean told her to get upstairs immediately, get out of her clothes and take a bath. In the meantime, her mother was going to burn the clothes outside. Claire had never seen her tremble as much, her face as pallid, while her father had woken from his nap after hearing Jean yelling, and he had turned pallid, too, when told the news.

After her mother had thoroughly washed her hair and ensured all traces of blood were gone, she told Claire she was to not say a word to anyone. She wasn't going to be leaving the house anytime soon either. She then left muttering something about child benefit and prison. Claire didn't understand her mother's reaction, but if she had thought no one was ever going to find out, a short time afterwards there had been loud banging on the front door. And now here they were with two stern-faced yet shocked detectives and a worried looking lawyer sitting across from them.

"So, Claire, we'd just like to ask you some questions, okay?" asked the elder of the two detectives.

Claire nodded. She knew where the questioning would be heading, but she had no intentions of admitting anything. She might get into serious trouble.

"Now, when was the last time you were at your friend, Michael's, home?"

She pretended to think hard. "Mmm, I think it was the other day. I knocked on the door but there was no one home, so I left. That was it."

"And you didn't go there this morning?"

She shook her head. "No. I don't think they really like me going there anymore. They have a new baby and they're always busy with it. Her name's Tania and she's really small and cute!"

"Right. So where did you go this morning?"

"Just out around the lake, then I went to see the animals and the pigs. I got bored so I came home, then Mr Forsyth knocked on the door really loud and was shouting at my mum. Then you came."

"So, you didn't go to Mr Forsyth's house at any time this morning?"

"She just told you she didn't," interrupted the lawyer.

Claire didn't like him. He looked mean. When he arrived, he told Claire he was there to help her and she didn't have to worry about anything, just tell the truth, but this was the first time he had spoken since they started questioning her. She wanted to go home already. Why wasn't he making them stop? She'd already made an excuse.

The detective ignored the lawyer. "Claire, did you like Tania?"

"Yes. She was really tiny and cute, but she cried a lot and didn't sleep much, so her mum was always tired, she said."

There was a noise from Jean that sounded like a stifled gasp. Her dad was rubbing his face with both hands as though he, too, was extremely tired.

"I think Michael was a bit jealous. He said his mum and dad never had time for him anymore and never wanted to play with him. I saw him looking badly at Tania sometimes."

It had only just occurred to her to use Michael to her advantage. If she was really clever, she could make them blame him for killing his sister.

The detective nodded and glanced at his colleague. The lawyer's Adam's apple was bobbing up and down like a yo-yo.

"Is that so? Babies require a lot of care and attention. They're completely defenceless, so it's normal Michael might have felt a little jealous. So, you think Tania was the reason they didn't want you going there anymore to play? That maybe they had swapped Tania for you and you were a little upset about it too?"

"A little. But Michael more so. He told me he was sad all the time because of her. Tania was the one they were with all the time."

Claire's stomach felt as though she'd eaten something rotten. All she wanted was for the detective to say they were going to go get Michael and put him in prison forever, but it wasn't happening.

"Okay, Claire. I'm going to ask you a question,

and it's very important you tell me the truth, all right? If you don't, and I will know if you're lying, you and your parents could get into a lot of trouble. Big trouble, okay?"

She nodded, but she didn't like the way he was leaning across the table at her. She could smell his breath and it wasn't nice. Why weren't they running off to arrest Michael?

"Good. Now, Claire, did you do anything to Tania this morning?"

"Me? No. I told you, I didn't go there today. They don't want me there anymore."

The detective shook his head. "I think you're lying, Claire. Remember what I said about lying. I think you did go there this morning, didn't you? Nice and early, after Michael and his dad left to go into town?"

"I didn't! I haven't been there for days!"

"You just told me you went the day before yesterday. So which is it?"

"You're confusing the girl. She just answered your question," interjected the lawyer.

"We have enough reasonable evidence to suggest she's lying. Claire, please answer the question."

"Well, yeah, yesterday, but no one was home, I told you. I don't remember the last time I saw them."

"We were just now talking about Tania. But in the past tense. You know what that means?"

"No."

"It means when you talk about someone that isn't here with us anymore. You were saying Tania *was* always crying, *was* cute and tiny. That tells me you know Tania isn't with us anymore. That something very bad happened to her this morning. You do, don't you, Claire? And you're trying to blame it on Michael. Yet it couldn't be Michael because he was out with his dad this morning when it happened. So why don't you tell us what really happened?"

Claire's stomach dropped. He'd tricked her and she hadn't even realised. And, of course, it couldn't have been Michael as he was now explaining.

All eyes were on her. Her mother glared at her, looking as though she might burst out crying or jump up and slap Claire across the face. Her dad looked terrified. Only the detectives bore no emotion at all. It was time to play act. She recalled listening to Michael and his dad joking about how she smelled bad and slept with the pigs. She thought about all the times she had been bullied and taunted at school. Within seconds, the tears appeared, and she held her head in her hands, sobbing gently.

"Mum? Dad? I'm scared. Did...did something bad happen to poor Tania? Whatever it was, it wasn't me. I wanna go home. I wanna go see Tania." And then she erupted into a full scale fit of hysterics. It was amazing, she thought, how easy it was to do. Her mother rushed to her side and for once wrapped an arm around her gently. It was the first time in Claire's life she had cuddled her.

"See, my daughter ain't no liar. She told you she didn't do it. C'mon, let's go home. Or you gonna arrest her?"

The detective looked annoyed. Claire waited for him to put handcuffs on her and tell her she was going to prison, but instead, he nodded and stood up.

"Okay, for now, you can go, but we will need Claire's fingerprints if you don't mind. You can do it at the entrance."

Her mother practically barged her out of the interrogation room, not saying a word. When they got home, she told Claire to go to her room and stay there. She fell asleep on her bed, giggling to herself. She was, after all, a very good actress it seemed.

A week passed. Claire was not allowed to go to school or leave the grounds, yet this didn't seem like a punishment this time. Claire thought so because her mother was being unusually nice to her. She ate twice a day, was given breakfast and supper. She even bought Claire her favourite packet of chocolate digestives, washed her hair for her with proper shampoo, came home one day with new outfits for her. Not once did she bring up the subject of Tania, nor did the police come for her again. She'd gotten away with it, she knew it.

But by now, she was bored being stuck at home. She wanted to go outside. She wanted to know what Michael and his parents were doing. Curiosity was threatening to tear her apart. She wanted to see their faces. Occasionally, she overheard the news on TV that her mother seemed especially interested in all of a sudden. When the news was on and Claire walked into the room, her mother told her to get out, so she would stand behind the door and listen. It was news of the terrible events at the Forsyth household that were a constant. Claire realised she was grinning as she listened to the reporter mention some of the grisly details that had been leaked to the press. A sadistic monster was being hunted, but as yet, the police had no suspects. This was good, she thought, although it also meant they hadn't arrested Michael. That was a shame. Then it cut to the reporter commenting from the funeral. Hundreds had turned out, and Mrs Forsyth had collapsed or something and had to be held onto to stop her falling over again. This really made Claire's day. She wanted nothing more than to burst into the living room and see for herself. She hoped Michael was howling and screaming like a little baby. His dad too. But she had to use her imagination instead. That was almost just as good.

And she had a good idea right now.

She left her mother watching the news and headed out quietly so as not to alert her. When she arrived at the Forsyth's cottage, she was happy to see the cars parked outside and the downstairs windows open. Not in the slightest worried about what Michael's dad may say or do to her, she knocked on the door. When it opened, Michael's mother stood there. Claire barely recognised her. Her face was puffy, eyes bloodshot with large bags beneath them. Her hair was straggled and unwashed, strands hanging in every direction, defying gravity. She stood there in her pyjamas, a completely blank look in her eyes, like a zombie, so lost she didn't even realise at first who was standing before her. She'd lost a lot of weight in that short time as well. It took several seconds before her eyes widened and her jaw dropped before the smiling girl.

"Hello, Mrs Forsyth. I haven't been around in a while. Thought I'd come say hi! Is Michael home? And Tania? I'd love to see Tania again. Can I come in?"

Kathleen stood there staring at Claire, her lips trembling. Then they moved as if she was going to say something, but all that came out was a soft moan. She staggered slightly, hand dropping to the side that had been holding the door open.

"Are you okay, Mrs Forsyth? You don't look so good. Can I come in and see Tania?"

"T-Tania?"

"Yes!"

"But-but she's d-dead."

Slowly, and to Claire's amazement, Kathleen's face began to twist, scrunching up, causing wrinkles to appear. Her lips twisted, and another soft groan came from her, eyes now glazed.

"Yes, I know. I wanted to see her coffin or her ashes. Did you keep them? I've never seen a dead body or a person's ashes before."

A louder groan came this time. Kathleen staggered back yet again, colliding with the door, which smashed against the wall. Her hand went to her mouth with an audible slapping sound. Tears started falling down her face. She raised a shaking arm and pointed at Claire as if trying to ward off the devil.

"Wh-what are you? How dare you? You're...you're sick. You killed my baby! It was you. Martin!" she yelled, and then the howling began as she slid down the wall.

Seconds later, a stunned Martin and Michael appeared. As did Kathleen, they seemed too shocked to react to Claire's presence. As if it should be her that was dead and not Tania. It was Michael who reacted first, the tears dribbling down his face before he ran off, too upset to even be angry at her presence. Martin was the complete opposite, though. After his initial shock, his face also screwed up into a sneer, a scowl, then utter rage.

"What the fuck are you doing here?" he spat,

foam forming at his lips as he spoke.

"I came to ask if I could see Tania's grave or her ashes. I saw on the news she'd already been buried. Can I? It was such a horrible thing that happened to her."

"You nasty, evil, spiteful, little bitch."

Claire said nothing, but when she thought he was going to tell her to get the hell out, he grabbed her arm and dragged her inside. She yelped, taken by surprise. He slammed the door shut, ignoring his bawling wife on the floor, and pulled out his phone.

"I don't know what kind of life you lead at home, what your parents are like, but you're sick. I know you did it and I'm gonna make damn fucking sure you pay for it. I don't care how old you are."

He dialled the police and explained what had just happened, then hung up. There were tears in his eyes now, despite the fact they were blazing with rage. He gripped her arm tightly to stop her getting away, but Claire had no intentions of trying to escape. She was enjoying seeing the horror and despair on their faces. Now they knew what it felt like.

The police arrived as well as the detectives that questioned her. She smiled when Martin opened the door and she saw them approach. Martin explained again what she had said, pointed to his wife still slumped on the floor, and wiped the tears from his eyes. The detectives looked equally shocked.

"Why did you do that?" asked the senior detective. "That was nasty and cruel. Why?"

Clair shrugged her shoulders. "I dunno. I was curious, I guess. I wanted to see her body."

"You already saw her body when you fucking killed her!" yelled Martin.

"Mr Forsyth, calm down. We'll take it from here."

"Calm down? Are you *serious*? She kills our baby daughter then comes here innocently asking to see the body? My job consists in analysing criminal minds, and this girl is a psychopath. Doesn't matter how old she is. There are plenty of similar cases of kids killing other kids. I want her arrested immediately and put in an institution. Fucking Northgate for all I care."

"Are your parents at home, Claire?"

"Yeah."

"Then that's where you're going."

As she sat in the back of the detective's car, she had to stifle a giggle. Michael's parents had been so angry and upset. She imagined how they must have been at the funeral and wished again she had been there to see it. Maybe one day they'd apologise to her for pretending not to be home or talking bad about her behind her back. It served them right.

"So, Claire," said the detective beside her, "you want to tell me why you really went to their home? It wasn't to see the coffin or remains or anything, was it?"

"It was! I wanted to say goodbye to Tania before she went to Heaven. Before they buried her, did they stitch her head back on again? When my grandmother died, my dad said they put lots of makeup on them so they look like they're sleeping. Is that what they did with Tania? Stitch her head back on and put makeup on her face to hide the knife wounds?"

There was a jerk as though the detective driving had hit the brakes then decided against it. She looked up to see him staring at his colleague in the rearview mirror. Some kind of telepathic conversation was going on between them. She caught the one next to her shake his head slightly. No one said another word until they reached Claire's farm.

They led her to the front door and knocked. Jean answered, still her pyjamas, a frown on her face. When she saw the detectives with Claire, she was visibly shaken.

"Now what you gone and done, huh? She been gettin' into trouble, Detective?"

"Mrs Peterson, we need to talk to you very seriously. We were just called to the Forsyth's property after your daughter was there saying she wanted to see the baby's body or ashes. That in itself is very disturbing, but that's not what we want to talk to you about."

"How many times did I tell you not to go there or even leave the grounds, girl? That's it, you're grounded, get to your room. Now! Sorry, I told her not to bother 'em. It won't happen again, I promi—"

"It's not quite that simple, Mrs Peterson. I think it would be better if we discussed this down at the station. With Claire present."

The blood drained from Jean's face.

She knew something was very wrong, but not what. Claire tried to replay the conversation with the detectives in her head again but saw nothing wrong in anything she said. But from the looks on their faces when they came into the same interrogation room as before suggested otherwise.

"Mrs Peterson, you can wait until a lawyer is present if you wish, but something your daughter said has us very concerned."

"I'll wait to hear what first."

"Very well. On the way to your home, Claire said something that leads us to believe Mr Forsyth was right after all and that your daughter has been lying all this time, as we suspected.

"She asked us if before the baby was buried, was her head stitched back on again and makeup used to cover the knife wounds to her face. Mrs Peterson, that information was not released to the press. The only people who knew Tania had been decapitated were her parents and us. Your daughter could not possibly have known unless she is the one that did it."

Claire watched as her mother's eyes widened and her jaw dropped, suddenly pallid. She wanted to slap her own face. *How could I have been so stupid*? she wondered. Thinking that she was being clever and funny, she had given away the fact she killed Tania.

"Mummy? That's not true! I heard it somewhere! It wasn't me. Take me home. I wanna go home!"

She forced the tears again and ran to hug her mother, but deep down, she knew she wasn't going home. And she was right.

Three months and a birthday later, after multiple tests and interviews with a whole host of child psychiatrists, Claire was sentenced to a specialist centre for children at least until she reached the age of eighteen. Being under ten years old, she couldn't be held criminally responsible for her actions. She was asked about her parents, if they beat or abused her, but she refused to answer their questions. When she said goodbye to her horrified parents for the last time, Claire shed not a single tear. But she did cast a sly grin at the Forsyth's as they watched her being led away.

***

We already know the major turning points were Claire's upbringing and subsequent abuse at the hands of her parents, but also the constant rejection she felt she suffered from everyone, specifically it seems the Forsyth family. This, coupled with the head injury she sustained, leads me to believe significant damage to the brain occurred, leaving her devoid of all empathy towards others, seeing them as nothing more than objects to be used to her gain. Even so, returning to the Forsyth's home after murdering their daughter with the sole intention of seeing the devastation on their faces...for a seven-year-old girl, this is truly unprecedented. Any other child would be in utter terror of being discovered. But not Claire. It's almost as if it she got a kick from seeing their misery in person.

"Why revisit? Weren't you worried about the possible outcome, which, as it turned out, was what got you arrested?"

"No. I wasn't thinking about that at all. I wanted to see them in hysterics, in fits of horror and grief. I wanted to see in them what I saw in myself. Despair. Knowing what it was like to lose what you most treasure, which in my case was a sense of being loved. Fuck 'em. They deserved it."

"But you knew they would phone the police, right? That there was a very good chance you might let something slip, as you eventually did, and you'd get arrested?"

"Seeing their pain outweighed everything else. That was the most important thing at the time, seeing in first person that what I did affected them so badly. If I have any regrets, it's not being able to finish the job. I had plans for Michael. I fantasised about scooping out his intestines and cooking them on a large pot and feeding them to him and his parents. I was going to shit in the pot, too, just as they shit on me so many times. Fuck 'em."

Chapter 18

Two months after Claire's eighteenth birthday, the doors to her home for the last ten years opened and she stepped outside. It was raining quite heavily, but this did nothing to dampen her spirits. All she had dreamed of since the day she arrived was this, of getting out. She had been subjected to an intense programme of rehabilitation, tests, and questionnaires almost on a daily basis. Having to sit in group and private therapy sessions, the same question asked again and again.

Why?

And just like the time when she had been arrested for the crime, her response was the same. A shrug of the shoulders. Fake tears. Begging to go home to her mum and dad, promising it wouldn't happen again. But she soon learned it wasn't going to work. There were other kids there, some slightly older, who had been there for years, and they had tried the same approach. She learned very quickly she wasn't going anywhere and if she got into any kind of trouble there was not much chance of her being released early either. Some of the other kids got into fights. Two boys got into a big fight and one of them had his arm broken, the other boy twisting it so far up his back it snapped. The boy, being over ten years old, was subsequently sent to juvenile prison. This was not going to happen to Claire.

As she got older, she learned to manipulate the therapists to her benefit, telling them what they wanted to hear. She even told them she wanted to write a letter to the Forsyth's, apologising for what she did. Her therapist thought it a brilliant idea and allowed her to do so, so she wrote two—one apologising profusely for killing Tania and another she kept hidden under her blanket in which she taunted them, asking them how it felt to have their lives turned upside down, to feel complete and utter desolation at so much abuse and horror entering their lives. She asked them if they thought they deserved it, because she thought they did. And that when she was released she would kill the rest of them too. But she never sent the letter. All her hard work and playing the remorseful child would be for nothing.

And now, here she was. Freedom was finally hers.

"Take care of yourself, Claire," said her therapist before she left.

"Oh, I will. I most certainly will."

She had been given money to catch the train back to the farm, and that was where she headed. The only condition was that she never head left into Belton and thus pass the Forsyth's property. If she wanted to leave the premises, she had to turn right towards Gorleston. If she failed to comply, it was back to prison. The real prison.

As she waited for the train to appear, heads turned her way, all from men. Claire had grown into an attractive young lady. She had not a blemish on her face, the scars from multiple cigarette burns and whippings from her mother barely visible, black, curly hair still reaching her shoulders, curves in all the right places, especially her breasts, and she was especially proud of this. It would be useful for future projects, she told herself. Not an ounce overweight, either; she had made good use of the facilities, the gym in particular. She smiled as men looked her way then quickly turned in the opposite direction when she scowled at them. Claire had had ten years to relive a multitude of memories, now able to comprehend things her young mind had been incapable of understanding when she was a child on the farm. And it sickened her.

She reached the farm and stopped to take everything in, memories flicking past like old secrets. A shudder rippled through her as she recalled some of the worst of those memories. Not that she had ever forgotten them, far from it, but the worst ones she liked to keep subdued, like a sleeping pet, only woken when she needed a reminder of what her mission in life was. Those were the ones that helped keep her on track, not let the horrific thing done to her as a child overwhelm her or, God forbid, allow pity and remorse to seep in. Besides, Claire had long since forgotten what such things were. They died along with her innocence many years ago.

She looked in the direction of the Forsyth's cottage, wondering if they still lived there or if the horrors of their own past had caused them to flee. She wouldn't be surprised. A smile brushed her lips, a tingle below as she remembered the slaying of little Tania, the howls of anguish from Kathleen and Martin. The nasty things they said about her behind her back. Fuck 'em. Did they know she'd been released yet? Had they jotted the date down in a notebook so they could perhaps come and harass her to get out of town or stage a protest down at the court that had imprisoned her? Maybe they even planned a little revenge of their own. She hoped this was the case. It would be fun.

Deciding now was not the right moment to go see

if they were home or not, she walked down the winding dirt track that led to Green Lake. More memories surfaced, like the bubbles on the lake; of rushing to meet Gayle, her new best friend, who for the first time in her life made her feel loved and wanted; Michael coming to play with her and the joke she played on him with the pig; the headless chicken flapping around while her father and his friends laughed; the slaughtering of the pig while the small crowd cheered and clapped, the woman swirling its blood in the large bucket. And as she reached the entrance to the grounds and saw the fishermen dotted about, she recalled other, darker memories. Her mother acting like the whore she had been, dragging them away like prizes won in a seedy contest, openly flaunting with them while her pathetic father watched on; the shed, which still stood, where she had spent so many freezing nights laying naked on the cold floor or in thin pyjamas, cigarette burns on her arms and legs throbbing terribly, teeth chattering so violently she thought they might break. She looked up at the decaying old house that was to be her home again and saw her bedroom window. She recalled all the times her father had sneaked into her room, getting in bed beside her and making her do things to him.

Her mother was dead now, victim of cirrhosis of the liver, and this was a shame. Claire had hoped to meet her again upon her release. But her father was still alive, somehow managing to keep the place running even though all of the animals except the pigs had either been sold or eaten. She was looking forward to meeting him too. Not once had either of her parents come to visit her. As far as she was concerned they died the day she was sentenced. Her father was nothing more than a ghost.

Claire walked down the path and knocked on the door. She knew her father had been made aware of the conditions of her release—to live an indeterminate amount of time under his watch and weekly sessions with a therapist to help her reconnect with the world again and talk through her emotions. Both conditions were fine by her. She had her own plans anyway.

The door opened, and someone that might once have resembled her father stood there. He resembled that man no longer. He looked to have aged thirty years since she last saw him, almost bald with liver spots dotted everywhere like animal droppings, just a few anarchic grey strands of hair around the sides and back of his head. He was vast and obese, too, so evidently he wasn't so broke and distraught about losing his wife that his appetite suffered. His face was like spaghetti junction, wrinkles everywhere, crisscrossing with the veins that snaked across his cheeks and nose, a tell-tale sign of a hard liquor lover. She could smell the booze on him as well as other stagnant odours suggesting his trips to the shower were distant memories and nothing else. But his eyes were the most telling. Aside from being what she guessed to be permanently bloodshot, fear and unease oozed from them like colourless secretions. He could barely make eye contact with her, instead preferring to study the floor, only daring to glance at her quickly then look away again as though prolonged eye contact might turn him to stone.

"Hi, Daddy," she said in a mock voice of her

younger years.

"Hey, Claire, welcome home." His voice was strangled as though his Adam's apple had inflated and he could barely breath.

"Thanks. Pleased to see me?"

"Of course. It's been so quiet since…since you mother left as well. Come in. Yer bedroom's exactly as it were when yer left."

She wondered if they'd bothered to wash the sheets since she left and guessed not. There were probably still cum stains there, her father's gift to her all those years ago. Piss stains, too, from when she'd been so scared and in so much pain from multiple beatings. Claire smiled and stepped in. The house smelled rank, of mildew and damp, dust coating every piece of furniture like a shroud to a wet corpse. She imagined her father sitting in front of the TV all day, can of beer or bottle of whiskey by his side, occasionally stepping outside to collect payment from the fishermen. If the house wasn't already paid for, he would probably be homeless.

She looked down and saw his hands were shaking, and she didn't think it was from the cold or withdrawals. She knew exactly why the pathetic man standing before her was so terrified.

"Thanks. Can't wait to sleep in a proper bed again. Did you miss me?"

Were his lips trembling too? Was he on the verge of crying? Claire wanted to slap the fucking tears out of him, but it was fun seeing him so terrified.

"Look, I…I really did want to come and visit, but what with yer mother ill and runnin' this place, I just…dunno, thought you might not want me to come anyway, so…so like, all those years ago what yer mother did. It weren't right. That was downright cruel of her. I tried to make her stop, but once she got a drink in her ain't no one stoppin' her. Maybe it's better she's dead. You can be happy again, forget everythin' that happened and start a new life. You…You'll be okay here. So…things went well at the centre? You're, umm, rehabilitated?"

She had to resist the urge to claw his seeping, worthless eyeballs out, to force them down his throat along with his testicles, but now was not the time. She'd only been out half a day and wanted to revel in her freedom first. Instead, she smiled.

"I'm fine. Thanks, Dad. I'm sure we'll get along great, just like before."

Chapter 19

Martin watched as Kathleen wiped the tears from her eyes then embraced her, hugging her tightly to him. They both knew this day would come eventually, but that didn't make it any easier. He knew perfectly well how the law worked in England, more than most, and until now his views had always been contradictory. On the one hand, he understood that a child could not possibly be held accountable for some terrible deed they might have committed, and to spend the rest of their lives in prison was neither fair nor suitable. But now, having witnessed first-hand what Claire had done all those years ago made him rethink his theories.

Several years beforehand, two young boys, around the age of nine and ten, had taken a smaller boy to an abandoned train track and killed him. They were eventually caught after CCTV cameras saw one of the boys holding the toddler's hand as they led him away. It was nationwide news, the general public in utter shock that two boys so young could do such a despicable thing. They knew perfectly well what they were doing, and it was not only illegal but morally wrong. As a result, the laws were changed so that children from the age of ten could be legally accused and charged of serious crime and sent to prison. Martin fully agreed on this change. The problem was that Claire had only been seven, and it was only because of the sheer carnage and mutilation carried out she hadn't got away with it completely. But now, today, she was free.

Their little baby was buried in a coffin so small

another might have thought they were burying their cat, while Claire was now free to live and enjoy her life again. It wasn't fair.

"It's okay, honey. That little bitch won't be out for long. Someone will recognise her and give her the kind of justice she really deserves. That or she'll end up in prison for sure. People like her cannot be rehabilitated. She was born a monster and will die one too."

Kathleen was too distraught to reply. She buried her face in his shirt and continued sobbing. Martin shook his head. Despite everything Claire did, something tugged at Martin's heart when he suggested or insinuated justice should be carried out personally when the criminal system failed. It was everything he was against and why he wanted to become a criminal psychologist in the first place. Justice had failed too many times. Innocent people had been hung back in the day the death penalty still existed. Guilty people were never charged because they had found a way to fool the system, pleading insanity to avoid going to prison, perhaps being awarded a short stay at Northgate Hospital for the Mentally Impaired instead. Families were destroyed, lives ruined, all because psychologists and psychiatrists couldn't agree on how to prove whether a person was aware of their actions or not.

His own sister had been stabbed to death one night while working at a late-night supermarket when she was just nineteen. The killer, who had been there to rob the place, had managed to avoid life imprisonment because his barrister successfully argued an insanity plea. Six months after being released from Northgate, the man killed yet again, stabbing his victim thirty-one times in the face and neck. It was too late to save both victims but not too late for Martin to make a decision. He applied to enter law school, specifically criminal psychology, determined to make a difference. And yet, some twenty years later, here he was with his wife sobbing her eyes out in his arms, while Michael had virtually become a recluse, avoiding all social contact with anyone except a very small circle of friends, and suffered anxiety issues. All thanks to a girl who was now in the prime of her life, ready to start a new one.

Michael came down the stairs after hearing his mother crying. Martin felt just as bad for him too. It was as if something died in him after his sister was murdered. He stopped growing like other kids, as though his body had given up the fight, below the average height for a sixteen-year-old and well below a healthy weight, all skin and bones, and an unnatural pallidity to his skin, as though he suffered some incurable illness. He didn't stop wetting the bed until he was thirteen, and even now Martin sometimes woke to the sound of Michael crying in his sleep. He had needed a therapist, too, suffering terrible nightmares where he was in the kitchen watching Claire mutilate and decapitate Tania while he could only watch on helpless. He said he often woke to the sound of Tania crying. Sometimes he heard it when he was awake. His eyes were constantly bloodshot and lifeless, all light repelled as if something very dark lived inside him. Michael was sixteen but could have passed for a very ill forty-something.

Kathleen didn't fare much better. It had been her dream to have two children, preferably a boy and girl, so when they were told the baby inside her was a girl, Martin had never seen her so happy. Neither ever said anything to Michael, of course, but Martin knew that secretly Kathleen had wanted her first-born to be a girl. And then along she came a few years later.

Since her death, Kathleen had enough pills in her medicine cabinet to open a pharmacy. Martin wasn't too sure what most of them were, but he guessed they were all variants of anti-depressants, anti-anxiety, and sleeping pills. She, too, sometimes awoke screaming or crying. She visited her therapist enough times during the week to pay for the man's yearly holiday just by herself, and when she wasn't there she was most likely to be found by Tania's gravestone. It had been six months before she could practically get out of bed, at first, until Martin convinced her to seek therapy, but even now, although she tried to be there for Michael, she struggled. She gave up looking after herself, letting her hair grow long and wild. She stopped eating, too, so a once perfect figure now resembled a starving one. Martin had done everything he could to bring them all together, but it had been hard. He needed to work longer hours to finance Kathleen's therapy sessions and keep a roof over their head yet wanted to be with them as much as possible. And then, just when it seemed Kathleen was finally growing out of her near-vegetative state and starting to take more care of herself, and they'd taken a much-needed holiday to Spain, they got the news Claire had been released.

It was wrong. All of it. They had done nothing to deserve such cruelty; all they had done had been to allow the little girl into their home, guessing she came from a broken family, and this had been their reward. All his efforts to reunite his family, grow strong again together, work to move forward with their lives as a unit, had been for nothing. He even tentatively suggested a few months ago, when Kathleen was slowly returning to the person she had once been, that they might like to try for a girl again, and she said she'd think about it. It was the most promising thing Martin had seen or heard from his family since Tania's death.

It went against everything Martin stood for, but Claire couldn't be allowed to lead her life freely while their lives crumbled around them. There was no justice in that. It hadn't been one defenceless baby who died that day but four people.

"It's okay, honey. Everything's going to be okay."

"How can you say that?!" She pushed herself away from him as though he'd been hurting her. "How can you say everything will be okay when that sick, little bitch is out there, walking around freely, enjoying life again? Nothing will ever be okay. Every day she is out there is a day too much, while my baby lies in a grave. They should have brought back hanging for the likes of her. I don't give a shit she was only seven when she did it. She's evil. A monster. What...what do I do if I ever bump into her in the streets? Have you thought about that? She might have gone back to that fucking house she grew up in. She could be just down the road from us right now!"

Martin didn't say anything, but he had a very good idea that was exactly where she was. Part of her condition for release would be having to stay somewhere they could contact her, and he didn't think any aunts or relatives would have wanted her. Claire's release had been kept secret, but thanks to contacts he had in the right places he'd been given the news.

Martin held his wife tight again and gently promised that Claire was never going to bump into any of them. He'd make sure of that.

Chapter 20

Kenny wasn't in very good health on the inside either. Years of alcohol and nicotine had rendered him old long before his time. He could barely get around the house let alone feed the pigs or collect the money from the fishermen three times a day. Claire couldn't care less if he dropped dead that very minute, but they agreed that while she was there, she would do the chores instead. And she was happy to do so; it gave her something to do. Being stuck in the house all day or going for walks by herself was only enjoyable for so long before boredom struck. She visited her therapist once a week and told her whatever she wanted to hear and even considered looking for a job. They told her they could give her a new identity to avoid any issues with an employer and colleagues, but she refused. She hadn't even given any thought as to what she might like to do. Nothing interested her in the slightest. As long as she could stay on the farm and receive her unemployment check once a week, she decided that was fine with her.

After a week of freedom, reliving her past and considering the future, she decided it was time. Once she'd fed the seven pigs still on the farm, she did the rounds at the lake, several fishermen asking her who she was. She told them Kenny was her uncle and she was helping out for a while. Being a warm day for May, she was wearing a short skirt taken from her mother's wardrobe and noticed some of the fishermen leering at her, but instead of being upset or offended, she smiled. *Let them look*, she thought.

They can look all they like, and when I'm ready, maybe they can look even closer. Once she'd collected the money, she put it in her jacket pocket and headed off down the dirt track, turning left towards Michael's home when she reached the end.

She stopped by a large oak tree when she was close enough and peered out. The jeep had been replaced by another car, and the curtains had been replaced, too, but other than that it looked exactly the same as when she last saw the place many years earlier. It was like a flashback to a previous life, when she was young and angry with the world, despondent and lonely. Now only one emotion remained within her, something that had lay dormant all these years. One that only surfaced when she thought about that day, still able to recall in vivid detail the sound of the knife slashing Tania's flesh, the smell as the blood filled the kitchen, her tiny bones snapping like twigs, the feel of Tania's organs as they were torn from her stomach. And that emotion, that even now was causing a tingling sensation between her legs, was ecstasy.

Such was the heightened state of her arousal she hitched up her skirt and began to rub her clitoris. She was wearing no knickers, so the breeze on her naked behind increased her ecstasy it even more. Claire had started puberty when she was thirteen and had soon become obsessed with sex. She understood in that moment exactly what her father had been doing to her all that time, but now she wanted the real thing. She wanted it on her terms. For months she liked to lie in bed at night rubbing her clitoris, inserting whatever objects she could find into her vagina, until she managed to seduce one of the younger security guards. It wasn't difficult. All she had to do was press up against him as she flirted with him, and once she had a hand rubbing over his throbbing erection, he was hers. It continued for years until he was eventually transferred to another facility, but she learned something very quickly when she was sixteen. While he was fucking her, she liked him to do so hard and to slap her in the process. She made him grip her around the throat tight before she orgasmed, twist her nipples, and soon this was the only way she could achieve it.

Leaning against the tree, Claire reached her orgasm as she recalled the moment Tania's head came away in her hand. She dropped her skirt, panting heavily, then suddenly ducked back behind the tree. Someone was looking outside an upstairs window directly at her. And given the fact it was from Michael's old bedroom, she assumed it was him. She didn't think he would recognise her after all these years and couldn't care less if he spotted her toying with herself, but what surprised her the most was that he was still here. He'd been something of a baby when young, so she had half expected him to have left after all the carnage he'd witnessed. She wondered if he suffered nightmares from it or required a child psychiatrist to help him cope. Maybe she'd ask him one day.

She dared to peek out again, and this time there was no one there. It didn't matter; she'd achieved what she set out to do.

She recalled the day she overheard him and his father saying how she smelled like and perhaps slept with the pigs.

"You'll be sleeping with pigs soon, Michael. You

and your pig parents."

Claire turned and headed back to the lake.

For the rest of the afternoon, she laid on her bed (she had, indeed, had to change the sheets thanks to the numerous, suspicious-looking stains) and reminisced on what happened earlier. While she was confident Michael hadn't recognised her, she would still have to be careful. She didn't need a lynch mob turning up on her doorstep and forcing her out. She had nowhere else to go, for one thing, and besides, she had things to take care of.

Claire had an hour's nap then got up to collect from the fishermen who might have turned up for an afternoon's fishing.

Once again, heads turned her way as she circled the lake. It wasn't a very big lake, but from what she understood many of the fish in it were pretty big, especially the carp, and dedicated fishermen would spend all day or night trying to catch the elusive creatures. Some of the men were napping on their chairs, others reading, others apparently zoned out, staring at the water as if something might suddenly jump out. She had just about completed a full circle of the lake when she saw someone who hadn't been there earlier. He looked to be in his late forties and evidently had no shame when it came to glaring at her legs and breasts. Ignoring his perverted stares, she smiled, said hello, and wrote him a receipt for payment.

"So, who are you then? Why haven't I seen you around here before? With legs like that, I should have seen you comin' a mile off."

"I'm staying here with my uncle for a while, helping out."

"Well, that's a great catch then, innit? Better than anything I caught all day. What's yer name?"

"Angela," she said quickly.

"Angela, huh? I guess you really are an angel, ain't yer. Fitting."

The man turned and picked up a dead fish he kept in a cool box. It was quite big and slippery, too, easily requiring two hands to pick it up. She was about to leave before the man got too cocky with her when she stopped. He pulled out a knife and made a long slit in its belly, the guts popping out and making a squelching sound as he pulled them. Then he cut its head off and dropped it on the ground. Its large, silver eyes looked up at her, and she was instantly reminded of Tania doing the same after being decapitated, of seeing the pig having its stomach cut open and the warm, coppery smell of its intestines and organs cut out. She shifted on her feet, a familiar tingle returning again.

"So, you got a boyfriend, husband, or anything? Someone like you gotta have. Someone like you gets it all the time, don't yer? Probably just has to whistle and they all come runnin'. Bet I could make you happy. Sometimes yer need a man with experience to show yer a few things."

"Man with experience, eh? I've had plenty of experience with older men. Just ask my dad."

The man looked confused, unsure whether to laugh or not.

She was wet between her legs, adrenaline rushing like a drug fix. She hadn't planned on doing so yet, but the urges she had now would not go away. As though someone had taken over her senses, her self-control, her focus was on one thing and one thing alone.

"So, you wanna come in for a coffee? Or something else?"

Chapter 21

Michael had heard his mother sobbing downstairs and then yelling at his father, so he stayed in his room. From here, he could hear what they had been discussing, the moment he had been dreading all his life. Claire had been released, and somehow his father had been made aware of it. She was out there somewhere, free to start all over again, while his baby sister lay in a tiny, wooden box.

Years of therapy had failed to cure his principal issue: that Tania had died because of him. It was his fault and his alone. It didn't matter that they tried to explain to him that Claire had come from a broken home, had probably been abused and beaten on multiple occasions, and was sick in the head. He understood all that on some subconscious level, but to him it made no difference. If he had stopped allowing Claire into his home, try to be something of a friend to her when he should have known better, none of this would have happened.

He should have stopped it the day she tricked him into going into the pig pen. He had seen something in her eyes, something he didn't like. His sports teacher had the same look—as though he was getting great pleasure from making the kids suffer by having them run around the school field so many times. There would be a smirk on his face, as well, as they panted and sweated. Claire's expression had been the same; she was getting a kick out of his terror and panic. That should have been the sign to keep well away from her. When she started turning up at his house every day, he should have told his parents not to let her in. She was nasty and cruel. And then when Tania had been born, he knew she was jealous that all the fuss and attention would be directed at the baby. He'd seen the way she looked at her that day, a look of utter hatred on her little face.

But he said nothing, perhaps deep down because he was scared of her, of what she might do to him again if she found out. And look what had happened. The scene in the kitchen when he burst in and saw her remains strewn about everywhere, little pieces of her dotted about like a doll torn to shreds in a childish tantrum, the blood still dripping down the walls, had never left him. He had ran to his room and hid under the bed for hours, his trousers soaked in urine, body shaking violently, until his father finally came for him. And it wasn't until Tania's funeral he found the courage to leave his room, convinced Claire was coming for him too, just as she did in his nightmares. The nightmares he still suffered all these years later.

Michael hadn't gone to the court case, but he was told when his parents returned home that Claire would never be free again. What she had done was so terrible she would stay in prison until she died. She was an evil little girl with something wrong in her head, and they would never let her out.

But they had been wrong.

And it hadn't stopped there.

Last week, when informed of her release, his dad had promised him she would never be allowed anywhere near them. She would be given a new identity and sent off far, far away so they never had to run the risk of bumping into her. If that was the case, why was it just ten minutes ago there had been a young woman about his age staring up at his window from behind a tree? A woman that looked very suspiciously like Claire, rubbing her belly or something furiously.

Shocked, he had jumped back, almost collapsing on the bed before sitting down on it. His brain was scrambled, more so than it usually was. There was no way. It was just a passer-by who had stopped for some reason on her way to the village or perhaps taking her dog for a walk. Happened all the time. There were quite a few cottages dotted about. He tried to tell himself several likely scenarios, and while all were perfectly feasible, he knew the real truth. He would recognise those eyes anywhere.

His hands shaking, mind reeling, he didn't know what to do or think. In that brief instance, he had been so shocked and terrified his bladder almost betrayed him. He took deep breaths, willed his heart to slow down as he considered his options. First, confirmation. Peek out the window again and see if she's still there. If so, run down to his father and tell him to phone the police. She must have some kind of restraining order, so she would be arrested again. Yes, good idea.

He got on his hands and knees and crawled to the window. Peeking only as much as he dared, he quickly looked out and dropped back down again. She was gone. This time, he dared to stand up and pull the curtain back. Michael looked both left and right, but there was no one. He sighed in relief, but the problem was still there. Claire hadn't been sent to the other side of the country. She was here, very likely living on that farm again. And if she'd stopped by once, she was most certainly going to do it again.

His mother was curled up on the sofa taking a nap, while his father was in the kitchen. Being a Saturday, he had the day off work.

"Dad?"

He turned around and smiled, but when he saw Michael's worried face his smile faded. "Hey, what's up, son?"

"Remember you told me that Claire wouldn't be allowed anywhere near our property or us when released?"

"Yeah, why?"

"I just saw her standing outside our house. She was hiding behind the big oak tree and staring up at my window. I think she saw me."

"Wait, Michael. Are you sure? Because it couldn't have been her. Ten years have passed, you must have mistaken her for someone else. They wouldn't let her come near he—"

"I'd recognise her anywhere, Dad. I see her face every night in my dreams. It was her."

***

Martin arrived at the farm less than ten minutes later. He, too, had been both horrified and shocked to hear they'd let her back home, just five minutes away from where he lived. There had to be a mistake. Michael was still traumatised after all these years and must surely have mistaken the woman for someone else. He had been assured by an acquaintance of a friend from the institution Claire had been in that she would not be allowed back at the farm. It was too close to the victim's house. They would give her a new identity and a safe house to stay elsewhere in the country while she looked for work.

He drove down the dirt track, telling himself not to get too agitated until he could confirm one way or the other. He stopped before entering the large parking area, parking to the side so others could pass if necessary. Martin hadn't been here since that fateful night Tania died. The place looked even more unkempt and overgrown. Litter was dumped everywhere, the bins for such things completely full. The house needed a serious recoating of paint, large patches showing the brickwork beneath. The small pond where the ducks and geese had been was now a dried hole in the ground, the skeletal remains of birds and rodents in its place. Despite this, there were several cars in the parking lot, so the lake must still be an attractive place to visit for the local fishermen. He counted nine dotted around its perimeter. He wondered if they knew Claire was home again. When Tania's death became public knowledge, there had been widespread outrage. Villagers chanted outside the house, demanding the parents get out of their town, the angrier ones throwing bricks through the bottom windows. Journalists had camped outside for days, too, hoping to get a glimpse of the parents and bombard them with questions. Money must have been extremely tight, and not just because it was closed off to fishermen temporarily, many of whom disguised as journalists, too, because Claire's mother had indeed done an interview. For a national newspaper, The Daily Times, she described how she was heartbroken and shocked how her girl could do such a thing, that they were model parents and had never so much as laid a hand on her. It must have been some faulty wiring in her head, she said, because Claire had always been such a sweet, good girl and she couldn't possibly understand how Claire could do such a terrible thing. Martin read the article and threw it on the fire in disgust.

He thought of stomping his way to the front door and banging on it until someone answered. If it was indeed Claire, he would immediately phone the police and have her arrested for breach of parole, but the criminal psychologist part of him told him to slow down. They had no proof Claire had been spying on them this morning, only Michael's word which unfortunately didn't count for much anymore. Claire's lawyer would take one look at the anti-anxiety pills he was taking and his countless therapy sessions and the case would be dismissed. Besides, hadn't he told his wife only last week that he was going to take care of things himself? If Claire had been allowed to come back home again, it was because they deemed her fit for society. And if she had nowhere else to go, why not allow her home? In that case, if she knew he knew where she was, it gave him less leeway to take action. Better to be cautious, keep the upper hand while he decided how to approach the situation. It was going against everything he had ever been taught and believed in, but if he had to take matters into his own hands to protect his family, then damn fucking right he would. Especially now that Kathleen was something of her old self again.

So instead, Martin sat patiently, huddled low in his car, and waited. He didn't have to wait long. The front door opened and a young woman stepped out. He knew about Claire's mother dying and that her father had been living alone since, so it had to be her.

And as Michael had said, there could be no mistaken identity. Even from here it was obviously Claire. And as she headed in his general direction towards the lake, he saw her eyes, those same piercing, blue eyes that were so deceiving. She hadn't even changed her hairstyle, now just a little longer. She made no attempt at disguising who she was at all, as if she didn't care.

He watched her as she circled the lake, collecting from the fishermen. Martin's heart was thumping so fast he thought it might impale itself on his ribs. The palms of his hands were hurting, and when he looked, he saw they were curled into tight fists, his fingernails cutting into the skin, drawing blood.

"You little bitch. How dare you come back here after everything you did? You come back to bring more misery into our lives, is that it? Well, fuck you. If the system won't put you where you belong, then I fucking will," he muttered.

He watched as she finished touring the lake then stopped to talk to one of the fishermen. They appeared to be laughing and joking together, like old friends. Martin felt sick watching her. But his emotions became too much as he recalled once again the horrors he encountered in his kitchen ten years ago, and he burst out crying in despair.

Chapter 22

As almost always now, Claire's father was snoring on the sofa. She wouldn't have cared anyway. She was beyond caring or feeling embarrassed about bringing a man into the house. Right now, she could do what the fuck she liked, and no one was going to stop her, much less a perverted old man.

She never said a word as she led him upstairs despite his lewd comments and insinuations, but inside she couldn't wait to get him in her room. If her father hadn't been home, she might have taken him to the living room instead, faster, but her toys were in her bedroom and the thought of using them for the first time made her giddy with excitement. Better not to let the fisherman, Gary, know though, let him think he was in for a good time.

They entered and Claire pushed him onto the bed. For the first time since she killed Tania, she was in control again, and this was a moment she'd been waiting for for years, since the day she was taken to the institution. Adrenaline pumped through her, her heart as though trying to break out of its tight confines. She was nervous, too, as though she was about to lose her virginity, which in a metaphorical way she was. Gary was bigger and stronger than her; anything could go wrong.

"Get undressed," she demanded, her voice lacking all emotion, like a robot.

Gary smiled, leering at her as he pulled off his fisherman boots then everything else. Claire stood over him, expressionless, admiring the naked man beneath her. He was big, too, her lucky day. She gripped his cock in her hand and squeezed, causing him to wince. Even so, he was already hard.

"You like it? Big enough for yer?"

She said nothing.

"So what, you just gonna stand there admirin' or what?"

Claire remained silent for a few moments before taking off her own clothes. Gary grinned and nodded, taking everything in, chuckling when he saw she'd not been wearing knickers.

"Kinky, eh? I like that."

He had no idea.

Now that it was happening, she wasn't quite sure where to start so she straddled him, sitting on his face while she leaned over and gripped his cock, stroking it slowly but with no intentions of putting it in her mouth. His tongue on her pussy was glorious, though, something she hadn't felt since the guard did the same to her a few years ago.

But it wasn't enough.

What she needed wasn't coming.

"Slap me. Hard."

"What?'

"I said fucking slap me."

He did as he was told. That was better, her buttocks throbbing from the force of his slap.

"Keep doing it, don't stop."

He did so while he kept his tongue tightly pressed to her clit, and a few minutes later, she came.

But not as strongly as she wanted. She climbed off him and opened her wardrobe. Hanging on a clothes hanger were the same whips her mother used all those years ago. Evidently she never bothered to clean them afterwards because what looked like dried blood still stained the tip. Claire got on the bed, on all fours, and handed him the whip.

"Fuck me and whip me," she demanded.

"You really are into the kinky shit, huh!"

Gary entered her and slapped the whip across her back. He did it gently a few times, as though afraid of actually hurting her. She told him to hit her harder, faster, which he did. Her back almost numb from the stinging whipping, she looked to the bedroom door and saw a scared, bewildered little girl standing there, not understanding what she was seeing. She understood perfectly well now though. And when the first trickle of blood ran down her chest and onto her breast, she smeared it all over.

Her body rippled and shuddered before she threw him off onto his back. He lay there grinning, sweat running down his forehead, cock throbbing.

"Like that, do yer? Gotta say, I ain't ever done that before, but it was fun, right?"

Yes, it was fun. She looked to the bedroom door again and wasn't surprised to see the girl had disappeared. This was good, too; Claire didn't need her anymore.

"Close your eyes."

"Hey, don't you go usin' that thing on me. I wanna get beaten, I'll go to the pub and get in a flight."

"Shut up and do it."

Claire straddled him and put his hands behind his head. Attached to the headboard was a length of rope she'd tied there a few days ago. Before he could react, she brought it out, deftly put his hands through the loop, and pulled tight.

"Hey, what the fuck? I told yer I ain't into this shit."

"Really? It's okay to do it to me but not the other way around?"

"But you asked for it."

"So did you. So do you all."

She got off the bed quickly, before he could lash out with his legs. He began to writhe and squirm, trying to break free, but he wasn't going anywhere. Claire stood over him, enjoying his feeble attempts to break the rope, insults and threats directed her way if she didn't let him loose. Her whole body tingled, heart thudding knowing she was in complete control of a situation for just the second time in her life, able to determine another's fate while they lay there helpless. It was infinite power over him. She was a goddess and he a slave. Her back was still throbbing, and she could feel the blood trickling down her back and buttocks, and this only made her even more ecstatic. Mum had been right, after all. With pain came pleasure. As Gary was now about to find out.

Claire grabbed the whip, brought it behind her head, and as hard as she possibly could brought it down on Gary's still-erect cock. It was like a bolt of lightning had struck in her bedroom, and from Gary's scream, it had been a direct hit. She did it again and again, for Michael, his parents, her parents, especially her father asleep downstairs.

Now flaccid, lines of crimson crisscrossed his penis and surrounding areas, nasty red gashes where she'd missed.

"You fuckin' bitch. Let me go!" he yelled, tears in his eyes.

She brought the whip back again and rubbed her clitoris as the studded-tipped piece of leather connected with his mouth. The force was so tremendous it severed the tip of his tongue as he'd been about to scream again. Blood gushed from his mouth like a pig having its belly sliced open. She picked up the tiny piece of organ and swallowed it.

For a second, Gary stopped struggling and screaming, incapable of understanding what just happened. He resumed again when she brought the whip down on his eyes, slicing them open, essentially gutting them.

"Roar like a pig, Gary. I wanna hear you scream like a pig."

Whether he was trying to comply or not she didn't know, but it seemed he was most certainly trying to do so.

"Someone help!" he tried howled, body rocking violently as he thrashed in agony, blood streaming from his broken mouth and his gutted eyes.

Claire decided to help him.

She was in full swing now, enjoying every second of being in control, finally able to do what the fuck she wanted, and no one was going to punish her for it. Aside from her mother and the other girls at school when a child, it had principally been men and boys that made her wish she was dead, that made her feel like something was wrong with her.

But not anymore.

She thought of one man in particular who had contributed to this new change in her. Claire dropped the whip and opened the drawer in the bedside table. She pulled out the cleaver she'd stolen from the kitchen, raised it above her head, and brought it down on Gary's mutilated penis.

It not only severed it easily but embedded itself deep in his body. The penis dropped onto the bed, a tiny, worm-like thing, so insignificant now, so destructive and deadly when alive. She picked it up and placed it in Gary's mouth, teasing his smashed lips and wondering if the same wave of exhilaration and eagerness ran through her father's body as it did hers now. She thought it probably did.

Claire had to use both hands to retrieve the cleaver, a great gush of blood drowning his legs as she did so. She used the handle to push the organ further down his throat, aware that if she used her fingers he might bite them off in revenge. A spiteful race, men. Gary began to choke, but with the handle stopping him from coughing it up he had no choice but to swallow it.

She chuckled then almost buckled at the sight of so much blood soaking her sheets. She wished she'd prepared better and brought a bucket to collect it. Another time perhaps. Right now, she was enthralled, hypnotized almost, by the sight before her, memories flooding like the crimson now flooding onto the floor.

"You deserve it, Gary. You all do, and this is just the beginning."

She sat beside him on the bed and stroked his mop of dark hair then leaned over and kissed him, letting her tongue roam over and lap up the blood still dripping from his mouth. She rubbed her clitoris as she did so until finally the orgasm she had been so desperate for was released to all its potential. She cried as her body shuddered, never having felt anything remotely similar, the nearest being the delirious sense of power when dismembering Tania.

It took several seconds for her to catch her breath, while Gary wasted away next to her. Claire's energy almost spent, she stood up, picked up the cleaver, and punctured Gary's stomach, the blade embedding itself in one of his intestines. She pulled it out then did the same to his guts as she did to Tania's, ripping them out as though pulling the guts from a chicken, stuffing as much as she could down his throat. Finally, after cutting off some of his ribs, she reached inside, found his heart, and tore that out. Daddy was going to get a special supper tonight to show how much she loved him.

Claire left Gary's body on the bed while she headed down to put supper in the fridge. The rest of Gary's remains were for the pigs tomorrow. It was only fair, she thought, that all the pigs be treated equally.

***

"This was the first time you killed someone again since Tania. Were you nervous at any point? That your father might come in and catch you?"

She chuckles.

"Nervous? I was fucking loving it. Seeing all that blood, my absolute control over him. I was that little girl again, finally getting my revenge on all those that had hurt me in some way. His screams made me even more excited in a sexual way as well. He was my toy and there was absolutely nothing he could do about it to stop me. You have any idea the power one feels in such a situation? My biggest regret is killing him too quickly. I should have let him suffer all night, like the next guy.

"As for my father, he would have been too scared to do anything. He could probably hear the screaming downstairs and tried to block it out, pretend nothing was going on. When that whip sliced his eyes open and all those viscous juices ran down his cheeks, I lapped them up. Did I tell you that? It tasted a little like semen, so I scooped those eyeballs out with my bare hands and licked out all the juices in his empty crater like a dog lapping water from its bowl. There were a few other things I did to him, too, I neglected to mention."

"Like what?"

I'm not sure I want to hear this, though.

"Well, I figured that since he liked to humiliate women, pretty much like all men do, he should know what it feels like. Don't you agree? No? Oh, okay, so my father had tons of tools in the shed from when he was in a condition to actually do any maintenance, so I went and fetched a few things.

"He was babbling like a little girl when I came back, and when he saw what I carried in my hands his eyes bulged. This is all before I scooped his eyes out and cut off his dick, of course. That was the main dish; this was a taster for him. I straddled him, and with the power drill in my hands, I drilled through his lips and teeth, shattering every single one. The reason being I didn't want him to bite me because after his teeth were all removed, I pushed up my skirt, straddled his mouth, and then pissed down his open throat. I could hear him gargling and gagging, but he had no choice but to swallow or risk drowning in it. That was fun. Fucking pig.

"I remember once my dad and his friends killed a pig but for personal use. A little piglet. They cooked its ears on the barbeque and ate them. They tried to get me to try a bit, but no way. I ain't eating that crap. Gave me an idea though. I took out Gary's zippo from his trousers pocket and set his ears on fire. One at a time. They sizzled and cooked just like those piglet's did then melted like candle wax. I don't know if the disgusting pig ever cleaned his ears or not, but it looked like a hell of a lot of ear wax running down his cheeks, too, all brown and thick. I nearly gagged, myself. How can people be so unhygienic? I'll never understand that. Personal hygiene is important, right?"

I truly cannot believe what I'm hearing. Claire's priorities are so wrong. She's grimacing as she mentions the ear wax yet smiling as she tells me she burnt his ears off. The pain must have been excruciating...

"Anyway, he kinda went into shock then, almost unconscious, and I was getting pretty hungry as well, so that's when I did the rest and went to make supper. My dad ate that heart like it was the best thing ever."

Chapter 23

Kenny grunted and rubbed his eyes. Something had made a noise and woke him up. It must have been pretty loud because very little woke him these days, not even when his bladder was trying to call out to him in need of attention, as was so often the case now. Since before he could remember, he drank himself to sleep each night, mainly so he didn't have to listen to his wife's drunken rages and rants. And even then, when she was really pissed about something, she would slap or kick him, try and wake him up so she could continue whining. It usually involved money and him, then later Claire.

Back when he met her, when they were naïve twenty-somethings, she had been different. The life of the party. The one guaranteed to get the party going and keep it going. Always up for a prank, a laugh, able to drink every man under the table. She was generally the first one on the invitation list when said party was being organised, and back then, not only did she have an extroverted character, she had the body to accompany it. And back then, Kenny was still battling with his conscience. Quite why she had fallen for him he never knew. He thought it might have been the way her eyes lit up when they first fucked in the back of his car and she saw what he had to offer. It also might have been when he later inherited the farm and she saw an easy way out of having to get a real job.

But in the long run, all this was entirely irrelevant. It meant he got to fuck now and again, more so in the first few years, of course, which helped, but back then it was more about having company, not having to run the farm and lake on his own, meeting other people. The sex with Jean was just a formality, a procedure he went through to keep her happy though it never satisfied him. Those first few years, before Jean fell victim to alcohol and drugs and started delving into alternative sexual activities, she did indeed help out, and he was grateful for it, but what she couldn't help him with were his other needs.

His special needs.

It occurred to him when he was around twenty that his needs were different than others. Before meeting Jean he had other girlfriends around his age, sometimes slightly younger, but no matter how sexy his girlfriends were or what they did to him, he struggled to maintain an erection. At first, at the promise of sex it would be immediate, but after a few minutes, unless he'd been without sex a long time, it would slowly but surely start to wane, despite imagining all kinds of things he secretly fantasised about doing to his then girlfriend. Things he was too embarrassed to say to their faces, of course. During those first few months, he assumed he was suffering erectile disfunction, which he thought odd for someone so young. There were other reasons he blamed it on, too, but it wasn't as if he was having sex with an old hag. His girlfriends were pretty, sexy, the type of girls that had to beat men off with a stick. As a result, his girlfriends never hung around for very long. The shame and humiliation was immense.

Jean was different. When they first started dating, she tried to encourage him, was patient, and it was her that suggested he try the kind of things he was too cowardly to suggest. And it worked for a while.

But as the years progressed, as did her abuse of alcohol and illicit substances, her attitude towards him changed too. Especially after he inherited the farm. Jean started looking elsewhere for sex and didn't care that he knew about it, often taunting him in front of others. That Claire was born at all was a minor miracle. And for Kenny, despite the repulsion he felt for his own acts, unable to stop even if he wanted to, his sexual needs were finally taken care of to an extent.

Because once Kenny became an adult, he found himself looking at girls young enough to still be in high school. When he saw a fourteen or fifteen-year-old, his heart would start racing. If she was wearing provocative clothing, as so many were inclined to do nowadays, he had no issues about his erection dying on him. One of his favourite hobbies was hanging around the school when it closed for the day, then rushing home and locking himself in the toilet while the memory of the girl he'd just seen was still fresh. When Jean had almost completely abandoned him to find her own needs elsewhere, he was hanging around school every day during the week. He would also wander around the big shopping centres where they liked to hang out at weekends, especially McDonald's. He knew he was sick, but he was powerless to stop it.

Then Claire was born.

And despite his misgivings, his terror at being caught in the act by Jean, he turned his attentions to her.

As she grew up, his terror turned to being confronted by Claire someday, perhaps some buried memory of what he was doing to her would surface when she understood better, and he saw himself in prison, being raped and beaten by the other inmates there. He would be shunned from the world for the rest of his life when released, forever on the list of sex offenders, condemned to die alone, in poverty and shame. Unless, of course, Jean managed to get their daughter killed beforehand. He knew perfectly well she was beating and abusing Claire in her own way, but he was also too weak and cowardly to confront her about it. Besides, he figured that what Jean was doing to her might make her forget what he had been doing.

As Claire got older, her attitude changed suddenly from being the terrified, bullied, little girl to more confrontational. He was just waiting for the day when she confronted him. Then she did something he never thought possible—she killed that baby. How and why she got it in her head to do such a terrible thing he didn't know. He'd read stories about abused kids growing up to be serial killers and killing and torturing animals, but he had not the slightest idea it might happen to Claire. Yet even then, despite his horror and then embarrassment as the reporters came harassing him and Jean all day, every day, the single most important thing on his mind was that he was safe. Claire would stay in prison all her life, never to be released, and his secret would be safe.

Now here she was.

He'd been informed and questioned whether he felt comfortable having Claire back on the farm, and his initial intention had been to say no, he fucking wasn't. If the parents of the baby found out, there would be a lynch mob on his door within seconds, and understandably so. He wasn't in any condition anymore to fend them off either. Jean would have done, but she was now as dead as the baby. When he asked them why here of all places and not the other side of the country with a new identity, they told him they sincerely believed Claire was completely rehabilitated. A terrible error from a little girl who knew no better. She would be given a new identity, anyway, and it would be impossible to recognise her after all these years. Kenny still thought of saying no for one very good reason, but he was old, incapable of running the place on his own and couldn't afford to hire anyone. Besides, Claire wouldn't remember the things he did to her, would she? She had more important things to worry about.

And at first, it seemed his terror and paranoia was unfounded. She hadn't said a single thing and had adjusted to life back home easily. He could relax and continue being a degenerate waste of a human being while she took care of other matters. So what was that noise coming from upstairs that awoke him in the first place? Whatever Claire was doing, she was evidently doing so with passion. He struggled to climb off the sofa and headed upstairs to eavesdrop.

"Fucking hit me, I said," came from Claire's bedroom, then a loud slap and a grunt. A man chuckled, the headrest banging against the wall. More slapping ensued, far too loud to be a simple palm slap. Kenny was only slightly surprised to feel a familiar tingle in his groin as he recalled all the times it had been him that occupied the bed with her instead. The slapping stopped, and he heard the man change from chuckling to agitated. He told her to stop whatever she was doing, and there came an even louder crack; the man howled in agony. Shocked and terrified, Kenny quickly left and headed back downstairs.

"*She's completely rehabilitated,*" reverberated in his head, the words from the head psychiatrist at the institution she'd been staying at. He slumped onto the sofa, screaming still coming from upstairs.

"Rehabilitated my arse," he muttered, his hands shaking as he contemplated his options. Claire was no more rehabilitated than he was. Before the screaming started, he had been about to lock himself in the toilet to relive past memories. Now he was wondering if he should take the easy way out, just in case. Because if Claire did indeed recall what they'd done together, it might be him up there with her instead. But being the coward he was, he knew there was no way he could go through with it.

Kenny held his head in his hands and sobbed.

Chapter 24

Claire knew there wasn't any chance of her dad daring to come in her bedroom, so she pushed Gary's body off the bed and onto the floor. It landed with a satisfying thud, what remained of his intestines spilling out beneath him, a squelching sound as he landed on top of them. He could stay there for the time being as she figured out how to dispose of him. If it wasn't for the smell he could stay there forever; it wouldn't bother her in the slightest. But her dad might notice it and call someone.

She thought this unlikely, too, but one couldn't take chances. Since the day she arrived home to the look of utter shock on his face, he'd gone out of his way to keep out of her way. The only time he really spoke to her was at lunchtime, and the uneasy silence between them was perfectly obvious as it gave way to brief spells of pointless small talk, asking her questions he had no real interest in at all. How was she enjoying her new life? Any plans for the future? Where did you learn to cook so well? She enjoyed watching him squirm in his seat, barely able to make eye contact with her.

She did give him the answer to his last question. When told she had to think of a possible future should she ever be freed, she chose working in the kitchen as something she thought she'd enjoy. With extreme supervision, Claire was given lessons on cooking with a goal to one day becoming a chef. She told them her dream was to one day open her own restaurant. And she was very sincere when she said it. They just didn't realise she meant a restaurant of a slightly different nature. Because even then, at fourteen, she was most definitely planning her future. And all that training was going to serve her perfectly right now.

After killing Gary, she had a nap, made herself a snack, and headed back upstairs. Once she'd removed and replaced the bed sheets–which did little to disguise the carnage beneath–she turned her attention to the dead body. Either they were stupid or ignorant, but the employees at the institution said nothing when she told them her primary interest was specialising in the preparation of meats. A lady in her late fifties took especial pleasure in teaching Claire how to cut and prepare them, the various sauces for each dish. Her father had been a butcher, she said, and had taught his daughter all the tricks of the trade. The other kids snickered and joked about her new hobby when they thought she wasn't listening. But she was.

Using the cleaver, she chopped off each arm and cut them into four sizeable pieces at the wrists, elbows, then between the elbow and shoulder. Next, the ankles. By now her arm was aching, so she headed downstairs, said hello to her dad as he sat staring at the wall in silence, grabbed a bottle of water, and headed back. The legs took longer, as expected, so she didn't rush, putting on some relaxing Pink Floyd to hum along to. Once the legs were chopped into manageable pieces, she sliced open more of the torso.

Claire sat back and admired her handiwork while memories drifted past. The smells, glistening organs and intestines, the sight of all that once perfectly-fitting material like an Ikea package, everything in its place. The only difference here was that nothing was missing, nothing surplus except perhaps the urine and shit that caked the back of his legs. Claire placed both hands in his warm stomach and started to pull. What was left came free, sounding exactly the same as the pig's, which made her smile. Even in death he looked and sounded like one.

Remembering what she'd been taught, she deftly sliced off the largest chunks along his sides, exposed his ribs, and hacked them off one by one then throwing them to the side like discarded trash. Then she cut off the head. Deciding what to do with it was a bit complicated, but she figured she'd think of something. Once she was satisfied, she put the unwanted parts into several black sacks and those that she needed for her purposes in a separate one. Leaving her father watching TV, Claire headed off to feed the pigs. Later that evening, she dumped the heavier parts in the lake, head included, knowing the fish would eventually devour everything, just as the pigs were doing right now.

"Bye, piggy," she said then returned indoors to prepare dinner. Her father complimented her on a wonderful stew with liver on the side later that evening. He said it was like she knew exactly the way to his heart. It might have been Gary's testicles she put in his bowl that added the final touch she wondered later as she headed to bed, grabbing her mother's old dildo on the way.

Chapter 25

Kathleen saw Martin's puffy eyes when he walked in, even though he tried to avert his gaze, tried to keep his head down as he went to grab a beer from the fridge. She'd heard him leave and drive off somewhere, and wherever he had gone had more than upset him. There could be only one reason. Martin was not the crying type, not even when Michael or Tania were born. Only when she died.

"Hey, Martin. You okay? What's wrong? Where'd you go?" she asked, grabbing his arm gently.

"Huh? I'm fine. As well as can be expected, anyway."

But before she could insist further, he headed off to the living room, switched on the TV, and pretended to be interested in the first programme he clicked on. She sat beside him, determined to get answers, certain she had at least an inkling of what was going on.

"So where did you go? You didn't answer my question."

"Oh, I just popped to the shop to get some more beer, but they're closed."

This was a lie too. Martin occasionally drank a beer when he got home from work, and that was it. And if there wasn't any in the fridge, he was quite happy to go without. That it was midday and he wanted more after the one he was drinking suggested he was very upset or nervous about something. He was hiding something from her.

Since Claire's release, the only thing she could think about was how unjust the world was and where

Claire was. Had she taken on a completely new identity? Had she changed her name and appearance, or did she not give a shit? Given the fact Claire had only been a child and the media attention had been massive, it made sense she would be given a new identity. Journalists would be fighting among themselves to find out where she was.

There was Kathleen, back on the anti-depressants and the sleeping pills, reunited like old buddies, while Claire roamed free, her whole life ahead of her. Kathleen visited her dead daughter's grave every single day to chat with her and bring fresh flowers, while that little bitch was probably having the time of her life.

"Have…Have you discovered where Claire is staying yet?" He'd promised her he would do everything, use all his contacts to find out, if only for peace of mind.

"Umm, no. I haven't. One person I spoke to heard she was in Wales with an aunt or something."

He looked away as he said it. Another tell-tale sign. Whenever Martin lied, even when joking, like when he pretended he'd forgotten their tenth wedding anniversary, he couldn't look her in the eye, mumbling his excuses as though he was too ashamed for her to hear them. Claire had been out long enough for Martin to have found where she was. He had contacts all over the country, other psychologists, detectives, barristers. He'd made it his purpose to keep in touch now and again with those in charge at the facility where Claire had been imprisoned. He told Kathleen that should the day ever come when she was set free, he would be the first to know. They promised him, they said. But they hadn't. There was only one possible reason for Martin to be sullen and withdrawn, and it wasn't solely because Claire had been released. He knew where she was and that he hadn't told her could only mean one thing.

"Really? Wales? Are you telling me the truth, Martin? Or just trying to protect me from the truth? Because if she's here, I want to know."

This time he did look her in the eyes, a brief flash of annoyance in them as they widened momentarily. "Are you saying I'm lying? I'm not, that's what I was told. She's in Wales living under a new identity."

He took a sip of his beer and resumed staring at the television. Kathlen watched him for a while, observing the little twitch in his left eye, the way he gripped his can of beer as though trying to choke it to death. She considered insisting, telling him outright she knew he was lying, but refrained from doing so. In a way, she understood why he was lying to her, but it didn't make it any easier on her. She knew he was just trying to keep the family together when it had come so close to being torn apart all those years ago. And when Martin had given her the news Claire had been released, all his hard work threatened to blow up around them. He'd tried his hardest to get her to stop taking the pills again, slow down on the alcohol consumption which had increased tenfold once more, but she couldn't help it. Every time she drove into Belton to do some shopping, she saw Claire everywhere. Every teen girl was the killer of her baby. Three times she'd almost crashed the car, convinced the girl she'd just passed walking along was Claire. The teen in the supermarket who accidently bumped into her with her trolley was

Claire, haunting her, wanting her to know she was back. Kathleen had grabbed the girl, spun her around and glared at her, trying to recognise anything of Claire in her face. The teen, understandably, had first been scared, then annoyed, and security guards had to separate them while Kathleen sunk to the floor, sobbing.

Whenever the phone rang, it was Claire, ringing to taunt her, to tell her she was coming for Michael next, then them. If she awoke in the middle of the night needing the toilet, the slightest creak on the stairs was Claire creeping upstairs with a butcher's knife in her hand. She'd confided all this to Martin the other day, who tried to convince her that it was perfectly safe, Claire was miles away, never to be seen again,. But it hadn't worked.

Even Michael was more withdrawn than usual, barely leaving his room, jumpy and on edge whenever he did come downstairs. Up until they received the news, he'd started to come out of his shell, too, like some terrified animal daring to peek out from its hiding place. Now, it was as though he'd regressed to the horrified six-year-old he used to be. So given all this, she knew Martin's reasons for lying, which simultaneously made her hate and love him at the same time. Knowing she wasn't going to get the truth from him, she rose and headed back to the kitchen.

Today was Saturday, which meant Martin didn't have to work. Before, they might have all gone out for the day, into town to do some shopping, maybe eat wherever Michael fancied, but that wasn't going to happen today. Martin might potter about in the garden to take his mind off things, and Michael certainly wasn't leaving his room—he'd already asked several times as to Claire's whereabouts, so Kathleen would have to go do the shopping on her own. Which was fine by her.

As usual of late, they ate in relative silence. It was as if the air was polluted with some chemical toxin that seeped into their brains and bodies leaving them in a constant state of exhaustion and despair. Michael didn't say a single word despite Kathleen trying to encourage him to come into town with her, that she'd buy him whatever he wanted. His response to her had been that she couldn't buy him what he wanted, then he quickly finished and returned to his room. Martin said nothing, either, making meaningless chitchat neither wanted to pursue. Once the dishes were cleared, she told Martin she was heading out shopping. When she asked him if he wanted anything, all he asked for was beer and a bottle of Jack Daniels, saying he fancied a tipple. The last time he drunk whiskey was on his stag night, a terrible hangover almost causing him to miss the wedding and subsequently assuring he'd never drink the stuff again. It made Kathleen's heart cripple inside her chest.

She left, having no intentions of going into town yet. First, she had something more important to do. Unknown to her, she parked in the exact same spot her husband had done only a few hours earlier. She had a perfect view of the farm and lake, but her car was hidden behind a maze of bushes. Also, exactly as Martin had done, she tried to imagine a scenario where Claire would be allowed back home, so close to where she'd committed the atrocity, and found it impossible. Surely the legal system would have prevented such a thing from happening. If it wasn't so tragic, it almost sounded like a bad joke, an experiment on behalf of psychologists to see how people reacted under moments of extreme stress and trauma. Well, if that was the case, they had their answer.

Poorly.

When they first met, she had been highly impressed with not just Martin's physical appearance but also by his ambitions and determination to succeed in his chosen field. He fantasised about unlocking the key to psychopathy in children and adolescents so the crime could be prevented before it even happened. Several criminal psychiatrists had already written lengthy papers on the matter, all agreeing on the early warning signs to look out for. Martin was more interested in the why's of the matter and if they could be cured in some way. And for Kathleen, who worked as a high school teacher at the time, she was enthralled. She'd known some bad kids at school that seemed to revel in bullying others, and nothing she or the headmaster did affected them in the slightest. She often wondered if they were now in prison or perhaps worse.

And when Martin finally passed all his exams a few years later, one of the cases he was asked to help with was that of sixteen-year-old Sarah Greenwood, also known as Sophie Blair. Sarah had been kidnapped not once but twice, and when she finally managed to escape—her father dead, her mother's mind broken as she languished in Northgate Hospital for the Mentally Impaired—Sarah had disappeared after a few weeks of intense therapy of which Martin had been a part of. Given the amount of suffering

Sarah went through, no one questioned her actions when she killed her kidnappers, but Martin had noticed something wrong with the girl afterwards. Rather than an intense grief for her parents yet relief for her freedom, she had appeared unusually subdued, not wanting to answer their questions or venture too far on her future. She said she had plans, but a short time later, after receiving a large pay out from her father's life insurance policy, she disappeared. Martin had been devastated, wanting to explore matters further with her, try to understand what was going through her mind now, but she was untraceable. Little did he know that just a few years later he would have another subject to think about. But now, things were different. He said he had no interest anymore in studying Claire's motivations and way of thinking. It seemed he had no interest in anything anymore.

An hour passed. The only movement was the odd fisherman entering or leaving, and she was already considering going into town, guessing that Claire's father was the only one living there, when she spotted the front door open. She had managed to half convince herself that Claire was hundreds of miles away in Wales, her husband was right after all, and she was being paranoid. Even if Claire was somewhere nearby, there could be no way she'd be able to recognise her. She would be a grown woman. But when she saw the figure step outside, the hairstyle exactly the same as all those years ago, she gasped and clapped a hand to her mouth.

Subconsciously, she had almost managed to convince herself Martin had been telling the truth, but as she saw Claire head towards the pig sties carrying several black sacks, another part of her already knew this was going to happen. The shock wasn't as devastating as expected, just a tightening of her stomach, her heart thudding a little harder than normal. She knew the moment Martin walked in this morning. He hadn't gone to buy beer, he'd come here, had probably parked right where she was now and saw the exact same thing.

Kathleen gripped the steering wheel with both hands, partly to stop them from shaking so much, but mainly because her immediate instinct was to jump out of the car and run after the girl, throttle the little bitch until she choked to death, all the while asking why. Why she had to kill her little baby.

From her position, she couldn't see Claire's expression, but the girl looked like she was thoroughly enjoying life, a bounce in her step as if she didn't have a care in the world.

Aware of the tears running down her face and tickling her cheeks, the memories of that terrible night came racing back to her despite her best efforts to eliminate them through pills and sedatives. She had tried to retain an image of Tania in her mind before it all happened, something to focus on, a pretty flower in a field of dead weeds, and to a point she had been successful. But not anymore. The sight of all that blood, her baby torn to shreds and cast around the kitchen like an old doll filled her mind and refused to leave, set in stone like a plaque, there as a permanent reminder.

Kathleen's body shook with grief, her vision blurred. The justice system had let her down. Martin had let her down as he sat there with his stupid can of beer and blatantly lied to her. The whole world was laughing at her behind her back. And this was what broke her.

Phone the police. Tell the newspapers. Tell the neighbours, her family. Grab a knife and kill her. Do to her what she had done to Tania. But while all these possibilities sounded justified and logical, it was only the last option that returned again and again to Kathleen's mind. Martin wouldn't do it. It went against everything he stood for, but for her and Michael's sake, it was the only feasible conclusion she could reach. Claire had to die, be removed from this world like a plague. And if anyone deserved to carry out the punishment, it was Kathleen.

Chapter 26

A week passed. No one came to arrest Claire for murder or suspicion of murder. No one came asking for the fisherman. Gary had come fishing on a pushbike, so she had stored that in a shed and burnt all his fishing gear and clothes, along with the stained bedsheets. For several nights afterwards, she relived the moment in her head, using her mother's vibrator on herself while whipping her body with the same whip. The first night after Gary's death the sensations and ecstasy had been almost as potent as killing Gary, whipping herself into a frenzy, drawing blood across her stomach while the vibrator was a blur in her hand. But the second night it wasn't the same. It was like trying to recall a face from years past, slowly blurring until it became almost impossible to see clearly. And after four days, the smell of blood having dissipated, the memory almost erased, the urges started to take control of her life once more.

It was like an itch she couldn't quite reach, annoying at first until it became a constant, incessant source of desperation. Three times a day she circled the lake collecting money, sizing up each fisherman as though searching for a clue. But despite her indifference to every single human that walked the earth, she found it impossible to just grab any old man for the sake of it. She was quickly learning there had to be a special set of circumstances to choose the lucky man. Now that she had access to unrestricted internet at home, she had watched lots of cases of serial killers and their methods. While many bore similarities, those that killed at random were not as common as she thought. Some killers preferred women that resembled their mothers, others liked little girls with long, dark hair. The majority focused on prostitutes for a variety of reasons. And while she had no qualms about picking up the first guy she came across, it wouldn't be the same. She thought it would be like trying a cheaper version of her favourite chocolate—helps to fill a hole but not all the way. And she wasn't going to waste her time and effort for nothing and risk getting caught.

But she had to do something and soon. She was getting restless. It had even occurred to her to grab her father, gut him and feed him to the pigs, and although this was something she fantasised about a lot, it would not be clever of her to do so. Once a week she would be expected to phone her parole officer to explain her thoughts and actions, and the same parole officer spoke to her father once every two weeks or so.

She could easily kill him and make it look like an accident, but where was the fun in that? Maybe Michael or his parents. They were definitely on her list, but again, she would be taking too many chances. Before their blood had a chance to dry, the police would be kicking down her door. So, what to do?

She was getting bored with life in general too. The monotony of spending all day on this shithole, collecting money and feeding pigs, while at first had been exciting had drifted away as well. Something was happening to Claire she thought would never happen again. Loneliness. It was all very well despising every man and woman alive, but this didn't mean she didn't possess some feelings. It wasn't as if she was completely empty and burnt out inside, soulless. She had needs just like every other human, someone to cuddle up to and watch a movie, take in a meal at some fancy restaurant. The last time she'd been to a restaurant was McDonald's as a schoolgirl, and that hardly counted. The money from the lake barely paid bills, and neither did her weekly unemployment benefit. There was so much she wanted to do, places to visit, to start living her life again now it had been returned to her. But, of course, it would have to be with someone who didn't enquire as to her little hobby. It wouldn't do to have a husband stumble upon her in the basement, dismembering her latest victim. Wouldn't do at all. She was young and attractive, and while her personality might not be precisely extroverted, she could still be fun. Since returning to the farm, she had kept her head down, kept out of trouble, and done everything her parole officer asked of her, but there was so much out there waiting for her. She was eighteen years old, and she'd never been to a party or nightclub, got drunk, gone to the cinema with friends, learnt how to drive. It was as if she'd been born late, stumbling out of her mother's womb after eighteen years struggling to get out. It had to change.

Bemoaning her lacklustre life, she finished breakfast, knowing her father wouldn't come down until she left, and went to do the rounds at the lake. As usual, and fortunately, the lake was busy today regardless of it being a Monday. Elderly or retired men who had nothing better to do or enjoyed the peace and quiet, not having to put up with the wife nagging at home, found the lake preferable. During the week there were always a few younger men, too, on holiday and looking to catch the elusive whopper that apparently lived somewhere below the surface. As a result, both old and young alike stared at her as she walked around, some slyly, others blatantly glaring at her breasts or legs when she wore a skirt with no knickers underneath. Which was often regardless of whether it was cold or not. She enjoyed the attention she garnered, imagining the men going home and fucking their wives but with Claire's face imprinted in their minds. Today was no exception.

She had almost completed her tour when she noticed one guy looking at her in a way she didn't like. She guessed him to be in his late fifties, and his eyes were squinting as though in deep thought, the occasional shaking of his head. He gave not the slightest glance at her body, only her face. She supposed it might happen one day, and it appeared that day had finally arrived.

"Hi. Any luck so far?" she asked as she wrote him a receipt.

"I know who you are," he replied, his voice oozing malice and contempt.

"Really? And who do you think I am? Maybe you've got me confused with someone else, because I haven't been here very long. I lived with my aunt and uncle in Liverp–"

"Bullshit. You killed that baby all those years ago. You've been in prison, where you should have rot. I knew your mother. Lovely woman. She died from the shame you brought to the family. I know who you are."

Deny everything, that was the ploy to use she decided when she left the centre. Admitting the truth or getting into a fight would only bring trouble and aggravation and consequently her arse in a real prison, so she smiled and handed him his receipt.

He threw it back at her.

"I ain't giving no killer my money. You're evil. A monster."

"I'm sorry, but you've got me mistaken for someone else. I haven't killed anyone. It was my aunt that died from cirrhosis of the liver, not shame, and I'm here to take care of my uncle."

"You ain't fooling me. You got the same eyes. I said back then I'd never forget that look of evil. It's you alright. How the fuck they let you out, and so close to that poor baby's family, I'll never know. But I'm gonna tell you right now, it ain't right, and I'm gonna go to the newspapers about it. You need to be in prison, not outside enjoying life again."

While he spoke, he was reeling in his line and gathering up his stuff. Claire had no doubt he'd carry out his threat. She glanced around to see if anyone was listening, but they were all engrossed in watching their floats bobbing up and down in the water. Knowing nothing she said would convince him, she watched him collect his things and head towards his car, muttering all the time about injustice and the terrible criminal system.

"Please. Please don't. I made a mistake which I've paid for, and my dad needs me here. He can't run this place on his own. Please. Don't. I assume you know my father too. He's a lovely man, and this would kill him. Have me arrested, he'll be dead within days. He's ill."

The man stopped to consider what she'd said. Maybe this was one of the men that helped him slaughter the pigs. A fine bunch of guys. He glanced around, as if checking for eavesdroppers. He opened his mouth to say something, closed it, then opened it again.

"All right. Yer dad's a good fellow. So I'm only doing this for him, not you. Doesn't change what I said, but give me a blowjob, I'll keep quiet."

Claire smiled and took his arm.

Chapter 27

In the same shed where she used to spend many a freezing night as a child, Claire told the man, Terence, to lower his trousers. She wasn't going to give him the satisfaction of doing it for him. The shed was pretty much as it had been, tools hanging from walls, sacks of corn for the pigs. Claire had done a pretty good job of cleaning up all the grime, making it more homely. There was even a bed, which she was sitting on now, Terence looking down at her with a slimy grin on his face, breathing heavily.

Once he'd pulled down his trousers, she pulled out his erect penis with the tips of her fingers, as though picking up a dead bug. As she put it in her mouth, she looked up into his eyes.

Then bit down hard.

He hissed, body jerking as the pain rocketed up inside him. He flapped around as though balancing precariously over something high up and dangerous. When he tried to push her away then punch her in the side of the head, she bit down harder and wiggled a finger at him. *Uh-uh. I wouldn't if I was you.* He took the hint and let his arms drop. Claire eased off the pressure. Under the blanket was a knife she left there soon after returning home. She pulled it out and let the tip of the blade caress his wrinkly, old ball sack. She didn't have to say anything for him to understand this message either.

"Please. Oh, dear God. Please. Oh, that hurts. Please let go. I promise I won't go to the papers or anything. I never saw you. If…if my wife finds out, she'll fucking kill me. Just…Just let me go."

Claire let his flaccid penis drop from her mouth. A deep bitemark covered the length of it, the skin torn in places. She flicked it as though swatting away a troublesome fly but kept the blade firmly pressed against his balls.

"Sit down," she ordered.

He did as told, whimpering like a scared little boy.

"Lie on the bed, arms behind your head."

"Wait, look, just let me go. I'm sorry. I never meant what I sai—"

Claire pressed a little harder, a dribble of some colourless secretion running down the blade. Terence winced but did so. Quickly, so he didn't have time for anything clever, she straddled him and grabbed the length of rope tied to one of the legs, bringing the loop over his wrists and pulling it tight. Then she got off the bed and admired her catch.

Just the thought of what she had planned for him made her body tingle. It wasn't supposed to have been Terence. He'd simply said the wrong thing at the wrong time, but he would do. Her initial idea had been to go to a nightclub in nearby Gorleston and see who she could pick up, but Terence had made the mistake of touching all the wrong nerves, and now he was going to pay for it.

Dearly.

"If you truly were paying so much attention to what I did or didn't do, you'd know I'm just eighteen years old, young enough to be your granddaughter. Do you say the same things to her? Do you have a granddaughter or grandson? I guess your type don't really care in whose mouth your dick goes, do you?"

"No, that's not true. I…I thought you were older. And I was really only joking anyway. Please, don't hurt me. I do have grandchildren. They'd be devastated if anything happened to me. I love them a lot."

"Really? Do you love them like my daddy loved me? He used to stick his dick in my mouth when I was a toddler, did you know? My mother knew and said nothing. Someday, I'm going to do to him more or less what I'm going to do to you. You pigs deserve it. That and more."

At this, and seeing Claire was deadly serious, Terence started thrashing about and screaming for help. She'd momentarily forgotten about him might wanting to scream so picked up a hammer and chisel and repeatedly hammered into his mouth, shattering his lips and teeth. They flew in all directions like shrapnel from a bomb explosion. His lips were split in half, dangling from his face like bloated leeches, giving the expression of a twisted, warped sneer. Blood splattered the bed, running down Terence's cheeks as he spat out the teeth that had tried to go down his throat. Unfortunately, it didn't stop his screaming, though, howling and thrashing even more than before. It was giving her a headache, so she grabbed the roll of duct tape in a drawer beside the bed for such purposes and quickly put a stop to his howling.

"There, that's better, you fucking coward. Look at you, you've pissed yourself. That's so disgusting. So much I'm going to have to punish you, Terence. Just like my mother used to do. It's going to hurt, I'm afraid."

Since arriving at the farm, Claire had been slowly putting together a torture and kill kit. She included all kinds of accessories at hand that she'd contemplated using while laying in bed at night. Some of the tools and things were used on the farm, while others she'd made herself. Upon release, she found it amazing how easy it was to access information on every possible subject known to man on the internet, much of which she was sure was illegal didn't know how it got there. When she started browsing porn channels, a whole new world opened to her. Women having gross and vile things done to them while apparently enjoying it, being beaten and whipped and humiliated, it all reminded her of her mother. Claire had been disgusted and turned on at the same time, grabbing her mother's old dildo and re-enacting some of the scenes she was watching.

She watched women being gangraped, whole fists and massive vibrators rammed up their vaginas. Given she had been raised in a very protective environment after killing Tania, she was completely naïve about such things, and she had become fascinated. All she knew until then was seeing her mother being whipped. She'd spend hours each evening watching the worst videos she could find. And then she stumbled upon femdom, men being fucked with huge, strap-on dildos. It gave her an idea.

In the bottom drawer was one of her own creations she'd been dying to try out on someone. Smashing Terence in the mouth hadn't given her the buzz she required, the sexual excitement she craved, so this was a perfect opportunity. With Terence still moaning and struggling, she pushed him onto his stomach, and before he could resist, she pulled his trousers and boxer shorts off, then separated his legs and tied each ankle to ropes attached to corners of the bed. He tried to say something, but it was evidently too painful to open his shattered mouth to speak. All he could do was mumble, spitting out blood bubbles as he did so. To help him, she tore off the duct tape then grabbed his bottom lip, which had been torn in two, and pulled it off, a squelching tearing sound ensuing as she did so. She held it up as though holding a morsel, watching the blood drip onto the back of Terence's balding head, fresh crimson soaking into the pillow. The sight of so much blood revived old memories, and this time something did stir within her. With the old man trying to turn his head to beg for freedom, she popped the flesh into her mouth and slowly chewed. It was like chewing a lump of fat, a little chunk like the dead pig she once tried after it had been killed. She swallowed it. Terence whimpered.

"You're a disgusting pig, Terence. You even taste and smell like one. Let's see if you taste any better cooked."

Claire took the metallic contraption and eased the tip into his arse. She could have used lubrication, but there was no fun in that. She found it harder to push in than expected. She jumped onto the bed and kicked the dildo all the way in. Terence howled, splitting open his mouth even more, the remains of his lips stuck to the pillow. And there was more to come.

The fun and clever part, something she was really quite proud of, was not the dildo itself but what was attached to it—two, long electrical wires with alligator clips she'd welded to the sex toy, stripped at the other end. These she pushed into an electric socket and quickly jumped back. The response was far greater than she imagined it might be. Terence's body jerked hard as the current was directed into his arse; he jumped into the air, his whole body leaving the bed. When it landed, he began to violently shake, his remaining loose teeth flying free as his head rocked up and down, back and forth. Something must have blown inside him, too, because blood began to seep down the butt plug. Wisps of smoke emanated from every orifice - his ruined ears, nose, mouth - as his body was being cooked on the inside. She watched, enthralled, for several seconds, not even aware she had risen her skirt and was furiously rubbing her clitoris. The sight of Terence's body being electrocuted on the inside, already starting to smell of burning flesh, left her captivated. But not wanting him to die yet, she pulled the wires from the socket before it could happen. His body remained stiff, as though dead and rigor mortis had already set in. Worried he might have died anyway she kicked the dildo again. He groaned softly.

"There, how was that, Terence? You enjoy that? I hope so, because there's plenty more to come. I'll be back in a minute. Gotta feed the other pigs."

She didn't, but she needed to collect something from them. When she returned a few minutes later, Terence was barely conscious, drool mixed with blood dribbling down his chin, mumbling something incoherent. There was no need for the ropes anymore, so she untied him and pushed him onto his back.

"Hey, Terence, how's it going?"

The shed stunk of burning organs or fat or whatever it was, but this didn't bother her too much.

197

She'd smelled worse. All she was interested in was that he stayed alive long enough for her to achieve satisfaction. The dildo still inside him, she pulled it out. It came out with a squelch, a slurping sound that ended with a plop as it released. There was something attached to the plug, too, something wet and slimy. Having no idea of human biology, she could only assume it was part of some organ. She pulled it off with considerable difficulty and slipped it into Terence's mouth, clapping her hand over it to ensure he swallowed it.

The room stank of shit, too, as it leaked from his destroyed hole. This wasn't a problem either. As Terence slowly came to, she raised his head, removed the dildo and poured a little water in his mouth, careful he didn't choke. After a few minutes, he started to come around as he groaned and tried to sit up, but the pain was obviously too much for him.

"It's okay, Terence. Lay still. You'll rupture something. And we can't have that, can we?"

He tried to say something but failed.

"Shh, don't say anything, fat piggie. Let's get you fed so you get some strength back."

She picked up the bucket she'd collected from the pig pens and emptied the runny, wet, pig shit down his throat and over his face. Before he could spit it out, she covered his mouth in duct tape again.

"There, that'll get you up and well in no time. I'm going home now to cook lunch for my dad. I'll be back tomorrow, maybe, but first I need ingredients."

Using her knife, she sliced open his stomach and rummaged around inside. It was warm in there, all his intestines and organs unrecognisable, some seemingly welded tight to others thanks to the strong electrical current. She grabbed what she thought might be the liver and sliced it off, Terence's legs drumming on the bed as he faded back into unconsciousness. She dropped the liver into the empty bucket and left Terence alone with his thoughts. Both she and her father were in for a real treat today. She thought she at least deserved it.

All through lunch, the only thing she could think of was Terence's body violently jerking with the electrical current running through him, the feel of his insides as she rummaged for supplies. She had a flashback to her youth; the feel and smell of the slaughtered pig's insides, of Tania's. While her father ate lunch in silence, not daring to look at her, she had been rubbing herself again under the table, almost having an orgasm right in front of him. But she wanted to saviour that moment when finishing off Terence.

She returned shortly after lunch, expecting to find Terence dead, but somehow he was still clinging to life. To wake him up a little, she squatted over him and pissed onto his face, the pig shit once again wet and smearing over his cheeks while running down his neck. Terence stirred.

"Hi, Terence. You okay down there?"

He failed to answer as expected given his condition. To help him wake up, she slid the dildo back in his ruptured arse and plugged the wires into the plug socket, but this time only for a couple of seconds to wake him up. He rocked hard enough to smash his head on the head rest and groaned. She tore off the duct tape, crumpled it up, and dropped it in his open stomach as though it was a trash bin. While deciding what to do, she let her skirt drop to the floor and began massaging her clitoris again, her breathing heavy pants as she contemplated what was to come. When his eyes opened slightly, she smiled and twiddled her fingers at him.

"Hey, you're awake! I bet you wish you wasn't, though. I bet you wish you were dead, don't you. Well, don't worry, you soon will be, but it won't be a pleasant one."

He whimpered, making grunting sounds in the back of his throat.

"That's it, Terence. I want to hear you squeal. Can you do that for me? No? Okay, I'll help."

She reached inside his stomach and started pulling out his intestines. A long string came out, much like the sausages her father used to make. It seemed impossible such a long length could fit in there. She wrapped it around Terence's head like a scarf, putting the end in his mouth. His skin was tinged a light purple as the blood and life drained from him. Claire picked up the electrified sex toy again. Just holding it made her tingle all over, her legs threatening to betray her as utter ecstasy rippled through her body. With her free hand, she pulled out a vibrator she kept in the drawer for herself, inserted it into her vagina, while at the same time inserting the other dildo into Terence's half empty stomach and past the rib cage, pushing up towards his throat, causing it to expand. She carefully put the loose wires into the plug socket and fucked herself with the vibrator until Terence's shuddering body began to smoulder and turn black, smoke billowing as he was fried to death, flesh, organs, and extremities melting before her eyes. By the time she'd finished pleasuring herself, Claire was pretty fried too.

Born or Bred

Chapter 28

The tension in Martin's house was bleak. Hardly anyone spoke to one another, and when Martin tried to make conversation with Kathleen, it usually ended abruptly and in some kind of argument. During the day, he spent his time at Norwich University working on his current case that would require him to testify in court. A couple had broken into the home of a family of four children and their parents, causing wanton destruction and terror before leaving. His focus was on the why of the matter, on how they could bring themselves to do such despicable things. But he often found his concentration waning, unable to focus for too long. Instead, it returned to Claire.

Claire, and his wife because he had an idea she suspected or knew more than she was letting on. Whenever he brought up Claire before—which was as little as possible—she would shrug her shoulders and change the topic as though she didn't care. Since Claire had been released, though, it had been the only topic of conversation between them. Where was she? What was she doing? Why did they let her out? Will she come for us? He'd done his best to try and dismiss her fears, lying through his teeth after discovering the truth about her whereabouts, and he hated himself for it. It was the first time in their marriage he'd deliberately lied to her. Kathleen had cried herself to sleep almost every night, resorting to the sleeping pills and Valium again to calm her nerves, spending prolonged hours by Tania's grave. The times he went with her, and when Michael accompanied them, he would have to gently lead her away or she would have stayed there all night.

But now, for the last week or so, she had completely changed. She no longer cried herself to sleep at night. The pills remained in the bathroom cabinet, and she was eating a lot more. Before this, he had been seriously worried she was becoming anorexic, her dresses hanging from her body like old curtains. The colour was returning to her face, and she was taking more care and showing more interest in her appearance. It was as if she had gone through some sudden metamorphosis from a soulless, broken shadow of a woman to one who seemed resurrected and eager to enjoy life. Maybe she had come to accept that Claire was always going to be a part of their lives one way or the other and she had accepted it, decided not to waste her time and energy on the girl anymore. This could be why she kept changing the subject whenever Claire was brought up. If only poor Michael could do the same.

The same could not be said for Martin either. It haunted him constantly, like a terrible secret he was condemned to live with forever. Everywhere he went he saw her. The sight of Kathleen huddled in the corner while pieces of their baby were thrown around like scraps filled his nightmares. But the worst thing of all was knowing she was almost within spitting distance of their home. The criminal justice system that paid for his mortgage had betrayed him like an old friend. He envisaged her laughing and thoroughly enjoying her new life, meeting new people, perhaps a boyfriend already, lying to everyone when asked about her history. Or maybe it was the complete opposite and in killing Tania she had unleashed a darker aspect of her personality, one which wanted to repeat the experience and was already planning on doing so. He knew from his research and working with psychopaths that they could easily lead double lives and control their dark urges for years, if necessary, until the right moment came along. Was that what she was doing now? Planning her next victim?

Well, that wasn't going to happen.

Since telling his colleagues where Claire was and imploring they kept it a secret, they had been shocked, unable to believe such a thing could happen. Like him, they felt betrayed by the system they had defended for so long. Several suggested writing to the Home Secretary and demanding she be moved elsewhere, but he told them no, they felt safe and were confident Claire wouldn't risk her freedom by intruding on them. This was, of course, a lie, because he wanted to know exactly where she was so he could carry out his own justice. The idea of getting caught barely crossed his mind, and the question about his own moral judgement was easily dismissed. He was nothing like the folks he interviewed and studied. They were sick individuals for the most part, for whom nothing could help them except strong anti-psychotic medication and being kept in a secure environment. The way he saw it and justified things was that any other father and husband in the world would do the same as he intended. If the legal system couldn't or wouldn't protect his family, he'd have to do it himself. Starting right now.

He'd told Kathleen that he had to work late—nothing unusual there—to prepare his court case. When he finished at the university that afternoon, he was nervous but also relaxed as he got in his car and headed towards Bradwell. It would be dark by the time he got there, and he knew from having watched the farm a few times on his way home that Claire did the last tour of the lake at nine; there were a few fishermen who liked to pull all-nighters. Martin wasn't going to rush, though. He knew from his contacts that Claire's father was ill and would be asleep early. All he had to do was sit in his car and patiently wait for Claire to do the same, even if he had to wait all night. He could see her bedroom from his vantage point, so when he slowly drove down the dirt track, he turned off the engine and waited, his tools beside him.

Martin had never been in a confrontational situation in his life, but he took good care of himself and considered himself strong enough to hold his own if necessary. Claire should be no match for him in a violent situation, but Claire wasn't a normal young woman. Appearances could be deceiving. Thus, he was still quite calm and relaxed as he watched Claire leave and do the rounds for the last time that night. Only his adrenaline pumped a little faster. Instinctively, he gripped the steering wheel harder, knuckles white. He heard a noise and realised he was muttering under his breath.

"You evil, little bitch. Enjoy it while you can, murderer. "

He watched her circle the lake, stopping to chat with the odd fisherman here and there and continue. It was pitch black over there, but the light from the house silhouetted her reflection. She was a monster gliding along the shadows like some mythical beast. It never ceased to amaze Martin how perfectly normal these psychos looked. They were the kind of people you'd happily invite over for a barbecue, or in Claire's case perhaps allow to babysit the kids. He shuddered at the mere thought of it.

Finally, she returned inside, and a few minutes later her bedroom light came on. Martin stirred, restless. Two long hours passed until her light switched off, and he sighed in relief. It was now past eleven, and Kathleen would be asleep already, probably on the sofa as had become her newest ritual. As for Michael, who knew anymore. Martin waited another thirty minutes, picked up the knife and rope he'd brought with him, and headed towards the house.

As expected, the front door was locked so he went around the back. That door was locked, too, but being a warm evening a window was open. Claire evidently wasn't too concerned about people breaking in. He was still calm as he headed up the stairs, which surprised him considering what he was doing. The adrenaline in his body made him feel lightheaded, needing to take deep breaths, his heart caught in his throat. He passed Kenny's room, heavy snoring coming from inside, then reached Claire's. He stopped and put an ear to the door. All was silent inside. Martin opened the door, his knife in his back pocket, both hands tensing the length of rope. He wanted to look in her eyes as he strangled her, wanted his face to be the last thing she saw before she slipped down into hell. Above all, he wanted her to suffer.

***

Michael grunted and opened his eyes. Disoriented,

he looked around the room, unsure at first where he was. If his nightmares were to be believed, he'd be in hell. He'd been in hell since the day his sister was taken. Then, as though given a slight reprieve, he had been given a taste of freedom only for it to be snatched from him again when Claire was released. Sometimes, most of the time, he wished he was dead.

He saw no future for himself. His closest friends had stopped coming to see him because the long silences between them made them uncomfortable. And with nothing to talk about except his nightmares, they were soon put off by that too. He didn't blame them; visiting a depressed hermit probably wasn't a very exciting thing to do. Even his therapist had pretty much given up on him years before.

When his parents had tried to speak to him about his future, his father had suggested he might like to follow in his footsteps, to try and prevent these things happening to others. He could become a detective, lawyer, criminal psychologist, anything, but the last thing Michael wanted was to be reminded on a daily basis there were others like Claire. He didn't need reminding anyway. His brain did that job for him perfectly well.

Finally aware of where he was, he realised he was thirsty, a normal occurrence from sweating and tossing and turning in his sleep. He usually made sure to bring a bottle of water with him each night, but tonight he'd forgotten. Groaning, he climbed out of bed and headed downstairs, turning all the lights on in the process. Michael was afraid of the dark, too, afraid someone might jump out at him from some shadowy corner. He grabbed a bottle of water from the fridge and was about to head back up when he thought he heard a noise.

It might have been the branches from the tree in the garden scraping the living room window, but it didn't quite sound right. He'd memorised that particular sound years ago after endless nights waking up screaming for his parents that Claire was outside and had come to chop him up.

Michael had no intention of finding out what it was. A chill was clinging to his sweat-soaked back as though someone had draped a wet cloth over him. He quickly made his way to the stairs, not caring about leaving the lights on, when he froze. Peering through the letter box in the front door were two eyes, gleaming in the light like a demon's.

"Hello, Michael. Miss me?"

Chapter 29

"It's impossible, Michael! She's not here. She's living in Wales, so you must have had another nightmare," insisted Kathleen for the third time. Michael was in hysterics in his room, refusing to listen to his parents' lie. Kathleen and Martin had woken startled at the sound of Michael screaming and bolting up the stairs and had come running to his room to see the boy on the verge of a heart attack. They eventually managed to make sense of his babblings and looked at each other with the same expression of terror. There had also been another expression on their faces. It was one Kathleen had seen rarely on Martin but knew it immediately when she did. Guilt. If she had been able to read Martin's mind, she would know he was thinking the same thing about her.

They both suspected one day this might happen. Neither would ever say it out loud, but the possibility had been lurking in the deepest realms of their minds like a deep-sea creature waiting the right moment to surface. They had discussed it numerous times; Martin had promised her it would never happen, until she discovered the truth for herself. And now, having to lie to her son was killing her just as much as the knowledge Claire had been on their property.

"I wasn't dreaming. It was her, peering through the letterbox. Call the police, tell them to check for fingerprints. You'll see!"

"Michael," said Martin softly, "it wasn't her. I've been told from contacts I have that Claire is not allowed to be anywhere near these premises. If she were to do so, she would be sent to prison for ten years, in violation of her conditions for release. It wasn't her."

Kathleen noticed he didn't look his son in the eyes though. In fact, he appeared almost as shocked as Michael. His jaws were set firm, hands clenched into fists, the vein on his neck taut like rope. So, it hurt him to lie as well. She wondered if it hurt him just as much when he told her the same thing. In that moment, she hated him again, as much as she hated herself, seeing the poor kid sitting there trembling and shivering, tears running down his pallid face like a toddler. She wanted nothing more than to phone the police and tell them Claire had been here, but there was no proof—a terrified teen's word against hers—and soon word would be out about Claire's whereabouts. They'd have to move home, not to escape Claire but the hordes of journalists and true crime freaks wanting the inside story. And while that had been her full intention when Tania was murdered, to get as far away from this place as possible, it had been Martin who convinced her otherwise. She wasn't then, but now, seeing her broken family like this at almost three in the morning, she was glad they didn't move. If she hadn't managed to fully convince herself about Claire's fate, she needed no more encouragement.

It took another ten minutes to convince Michael Claire hadn't been here, including Martin going outside to check for footprints or any sign of her, for the boy to go back to bed. As they left his room, they heard a heavy piece of furniture being dragged across his room. When they got back into bed, neither said a word, both lost in their thoughts until they fell asleep.

The next morning, Kathleen awoke to see Martin had already left for work. She tried to poke her head into Michael's room, but the door wouldn't budge. She could hear him snoring softly, though, so left him alone. Kathleen had plans for today.

She had a quick breakfast even though she wasn't the slightest bit hungry. There was a knot in her stomach, conceived of nerves, hate, and a desire for revenge, slowly consuming her insides. If she thought she'd get away with it, she'd carry out her plan right now. But there wasn't a chance in hell she was going to prison for Claire. She'd kill herself first. Once she'd forced her cereal and coffee down, she dressed, grabbed the car keys, and headed off into town.

As usual when she went shopping, locals stopped to ask her how things were. How was Michael? She knew most of them were genuinely trying to be nice, keep her in their thoughts, but she also knew she and her family were the hot topic right now. Gossip and morbid curiosity were rife in these villages. With everything that had happened over the years, it seemed they could never truly feel safe; there was always another monster ready to take the place of the last. They still hadn't gotten over the tragedy of Sarah Greenwood's terrible kidnapping, the girl set to be a published author at sixteen and who was now considered a person of interest for a series of brutal revenge murders in nearby villages. Kathleen couldn't blame her. Maybe they could meet up one day, chat over coffee about different ways to inflict exactly what these bastards deserved. One woman invented a type of cactus using a strap-on dildo, which Kathleen privately thought was brilliant.

211

She hurriedly fobbed off the well-doers, eager to finish up and get home. She stopped at the petrol station and filled up a cannister, hands shaking as she did so, as though everyone could read her mind as to her intentions. And her intentions were quite simple: she was going to burn down that fucking farmhouse with everyone in it, even Claire's father if he was still alive, because that son of a bitch must have known what she'd done and had covered up for her. Just like Claire's mother, using the tragedy to make money from it. Shame she wasn't still alive too. She would burn also.

Kathleen paid the attendant and was heading back to her car with the cannister in her hand when she froze. The cannister fell from her hand. She swayed on her feet, not believing what she was seeing. The fumes from the petrol were playing with her head, causing hallucinations, because it simply couldn't be real. Then she remembered Michael screaming last night and talking about monsters with demon's eyes.

"Hi, Mrs Forsyth. Nice to see you again. What were you planning on doing with that cannister? Gonna have a bonfire? And how's Tania after all these years?"

Chapter 30

Claire knew full well the petrol cannister she'd seen wasn't for a bonfire or in case Kathleen ran out of petrol one day. After visiting Michael, she'd made her way home, careful to cut through the fields so no one saw her where she wasn't supposed to be, and she'd seen Martin's car drive past. And because it had been drizzling that night, there had been fresh tire tracks at the entrance to the grounds, and no fishermen had either left or gone home. She counted. Besides, she didn't think it had been any fisherman that had entered her home and left muddy footprints everywhere, specifically outside her bedroom.

Somehow, before she even decided to pay Michael a little visit, they had found out she was back home. She guessed it wasn't too difficult given Martin's job, but she was still surprised they decided to make an impromptu visit and even more so that he had been traipsing through her house. And there could be only one reason for that: Martin had decided he couldn't handle having his daughter's killer so close to home. He wanted a little revenge so the poor man and his family could sleep peacefully at nights.

"Well, what about me?" she muttered, as she lay in bed watching television. "Did you ever think about whether I was sleeping safe? Whether I was in danger? You didn't give a shit, none of you did. My mum could have fucking killed me, and you wouldn't have cared less. You're gonna get what you deserve. All of you."

Whether Kathleen was a part of Martin's plan or not she hadn't known, but after seeing her with that cannister, she had to assume she was. Michael was probably so traumatised he wet his bed every night, screamed for his mummy and daddy every night, had tried every therapist and psychologist in the whole of Norfolk and still cried himself to sleep. Well, fuck him. Fuck 'em all. She'd stalked Kathleen one morning, too, following her to the graveyard where Tania was buried. She'd listened to her weeping and sobbing, talking to her as if the stupid thing was still alive. Once Kathleen had left, Claire crept over to the grave and pissed on it. She would have shit on it if she'd carried toilet paper with her. Fuck her too.

A part of Claire wanted to ignore them altogether, forget they ever existed and get on with her life, but another, the one that resided in the darkest recesses of her mind, refused. The thrill of seeing the horror in their faces after discovering Tania's body was something she had wanted to relive over and over. Killing the stupid, old fishermen wasn't giving her the satisfaction she craved so badly. She wanted them all to pay for what they did to her in the most horrific of ways. And by the look of things, it was time to do so, right now before they came and burned her house down. But first, they needed a little warning, something to make them think twice if they wanted to try something stupid.

One of the pigs had had eight piglets recently, and her father had told her they needed to sell five and keep the rest. This gave her an idea. She headed over to the shed where the tools were and, careful not to be spotted by anyone, made her way to the sleeping pigs. Once she'd finished, Claire went to the Forsyth's home. She knew the alarm system would be in place and switched on, but this didn't deter her.

One of the benefits of being in a young offender's institution was being with other similar-minded kids, all with their own little tricks of the trade they'd picked up along the way. One boy was particularly clever when it came to breaking and entering, picking locks, and disenabling alarms. When Claire was fifteen, she agreed to give him a blowjob in exchange for the valuable information.

And it worked perfectly. Claire quietly entered, closing the front door behind her, and made her way upstairs.

***

His parents were lying. Michael knew this without a doubt. He saw it in their eyes, the ways they were unable to hold his gaze for more than a second, the little glances between them as if they held a secret he mustn't know about. And he knew damn well what that secret was. He could understand they didn't want him even more terrified and traumatised than he already was, but he deserved to know. He might not leave the house much, but that didn't matter in the slightest. Claire had come to him. What if she came again when his parents weren't home? She could have some vengeful desire to kill them all. He'd heard about what happened to her during her childhood, and while he hadn't felt the slightest remorse for her, he guessed she might not be thinking the same way. They had practically kicked her out and ignored her, and a short time later Tania had been brutally murdered. It wasn't a coincidence.

The only thing he could think of doing was to hide a large kitchen knife under his pillow. If Claire came for them, he wanted to be prepared, and if she did try anything, he wasn't going to make it easy for her. The knife lay there now. It made sleep slightly uncomfortable with the large, heavy handle, as though sleeping with a rock under his pillow, but the sense of security it provided was worth it.

His bladder had woken him as it usually did this time of the night. He rubbed the sleep from his eyes and groaned, not wanting to get up. As always, and even more so now, he strained to hear for any foreign sounds. Michael had made his dad cut back the branches from the tree earlier so they didn't scrape against his window like some monster's fingernails, so all was quiet outside. All he could hear was the slightest rustling of leaves from the wind that was picking up and the occasional dog barking in the distance. There was still something not quite right though. The bedsheets were wet, as though he'd pissed the bed again, but he hadn't done that for a while now. There was also a smell in the room, like he had been hoarding all his dirty socks under the bed and the smell had finally become overpowering. Disgusted and embarrassed with himself, Michael hauled himself out of bed and turned on the light switch across the room.

It took him a few seconds to understand what he was seeing. He had expected to see a large wet patch on the bed, and while the sheets were indeed wet, it was not the way he imagined. There was something in his bed. He rubbed his eyes to clear the blurriness from them and tentatively approached.

And quickly jumped back, a scream bubbling at the back of his throat.

Michael quickly lifted his t-shirt and checked he

was okay, because the first thing that occurred to him was that he had somehow managed to disembowel himself. But he was fine, not a scratch except for a red stain on his t-shirt. Then he took a closer look and understood. Laying in his bed was a series of animal organs. He had no idea which ones, but there could be no denying what they were, in a thick pool of blood, spread out across the bed. A trail of intestines was curled up on the pillow like a sleeping snake, and when he wiped his cheeks his hand came away smeared red. The organs were tiny, he thought perhaps from a bird or something, until he saw the little, curly tail, like a worm. When he threw back the rest of the blanket, he knew what the intestines belonged to. Its little, pink body lay at the foot of his bed, missing its head, just an open, empty carcass with four tiny hooves pointing upwards.

As he stepped backwards, shaking his head, muttering gibberish, his eyes caught sight of what was lying under the bed. But before that he also inadvertently found the source of the bad smell. His foot sank into something soft. When he looked down, whoever had brought the mutilated pig had also seen fit to drop a shit in the middle of the room. As his foot sank, it oozed between his toes like butter, a slurping sound accompanying it as though walking through a field of wet mud.

In too much shock to even acknowledge it, he sank to his knees and stared, horrified, at the two, empty eye sockets staring back at him. He was unsure why he pulled out the piglet's head and looked at it, as though he'd discovered some disgusting new species of giant bug. Disgusting and shocking as it was, it was the carvings crudely cut into its forehead that made him drop it and start blabbering.

You're Next.

Chapter 31

The police came and took away the grisly remains after speaking with all three of them, although Michael was barely coherent. When his parents came rushing in once more and were confronted with the horrific sight, both had stopped in their tracks. They found Michael sprawled on the floor, shaking violently and babbling gibberish while covering his face. When Martin saw the intestines spread about, the head on the floor, he thought someone had dug up Tania's remains and brought them here as part of a sick, twisted prank, even though Tania was nothing but a skeleton by now. Only when he realised he was looking at a piglet's head and not a human's did it dawn on him what had happened.

He glanced at Kathleen, feeling strangely guilty for reasons he didn't understand. In the few seconds before they both rushed to Michael's side, she had the same look on her face, as if she was somehow responsible for this. When both grabbed Michael to hug him and try and calm him down, it was then Martin saw what his son had stepped in, originally believing it to be a thick pool of blood. He turned and vomited on the carpet, more out of horror than anything else, adding to the grim concoction.

"She's coming for me!" wailed Michael again and again. "She's gonna kill us all! You lied to me!"

He almost broke both their noses with the ferocity in which he shook and the way he waved his arms about. They both stepped back.

"Michael, listen to me. It wasn't Claire. It was someone paying a sick prank. I'm gonna phone the

219

police. Kathy, get him to the bathtub and clean him up for God's sake!"

But she seemed to be shellshocked, too, staring at the pig's head as though hypnotised.

"Kathy! Get him outta here!"

She jerked, glancing up at him with glazed, lost eyes, tears running from them as though trying to escape some new terror. Martin helped her raise Michael to his feet, the kid totally unaware what he'd stood in, traipsing it across the carpet and leaving a trail behind like some foul monster had risen from the sewers. Once they'd managed to get him in the bath and Kathleen ran warm water, Martin returned to the room and surveyed the damage with his head in his hands.

Deep down he knew something might occur, that Claire would want to finish off what she'd started all those years ago. It was always the case with serial killers, wanting to return to the scene of the crime, relive old memories, but he had also convinced himself that Claire had come from a troubled background and might have outgrown the hate she carried inside. Obviously not.

"I should have fucking killed you the other night," he muttered to himself, the sound of Michael still babbling nonsense in the background. There was another thing; if Michael was barely stable now, this was going to send him into total relapse. No therapy was going to wash this from his mind, the idea he'd been sleeping with a mutilated piglet all night. And now there was no way he could not phone the police without giving away what he already knew. Kathleen's suspicion would be immediate, and she'd know he'd been lying to her. He had no choice but to phone them and hope Claire had an alibi. Because right now, the last thing he wanted was Claire getting the easy way out. Prison was too good for the likes of her.

When they did come, the detectives were horrified, both looking as though they might throw up too. With Kathleen trying to comfort Michael downstairs, Martin told them he had no idea who might have done such a thing. A sick prank by kids, perhaps, but inevitably the questions turned to Claire. Had he seen her at all? Was he aware of her location? He replied no to them all, and while he didn't expect the forensics to find fingerprints, he knew they'd find her DNA in the gift she'd left for them. But that would take time, precious time to make things right again. Whether they knew where Claire was living he didn't know, and neither of the two burly detectives suggested they did, but it wouldn't take long for them to find out. Maybe tonight, now that the police had gone, he should settle this once and for all.

But Michael had other plans for them both instead.

They tried giving him one of Kathleen's sedatives so he could at least sleep, but he was too agitated, too nervous, too distraught. He'd regressed to that ten-year-old boy again, or someone born with some kind of mental deficiency. He rocked back and forth on the sofa, mumbling to himself, drool dribbling down his chin, peeing himself involuntarily every now and again, staining his pyjamas. After an hour with no luck in getting him to sleep or take the medication, which he spat out every time, they had no choice but to call a doctor.

When he arrived and Martin explained what had

happened, the doctor's words left him holding his head in his hands once again, hating and blaming himself for everything that had happened.

"Given his state right now, my advice is an indeterminate amount of time in Northgate Hospital for the Mentally Impaired."

Both Kathleen and Martin cried later that night as Michael was admitted. Michael didn't even seem to be aware where he was.

There was a tense silence between them when they arrived home, the only sound Kathleen's snivelling in the car. Yet as soon as they entered the front door and made it to the living room, it was as if an unspoken agreement had been broken between them.

"You knew, didn't you? You fucking knew all along Claire was back."

"Kathy, listen, I—"

"Don't you fucking Kathy me. Look at what you've done! You could have stopped this, but instead you've let our son become a...a fucking zombie! He's ruined. He'll never get over this. Why the fuck did you lie to us?!"

"Precisely because I wanted to avoid this! I figured if you both knew she was not only free but living just down the road again, you'd both freak! I never once thought she'd dare come anywhere near our house. And especially not in our fucking house!"

"You're supposed to be the damn psychologist. You're supposed to know how their minds work. If she was allowed to come back to the village, of course she'd be tempted to revisit. Even I know killers like to revisit the crime scene."

"She's not supposed to come anywhere near this

area. The terms of her parole were precisely that. And besides, it wasn't me that deemed her fit for society again. I would have kept her in prison the rest of her fucking life. It's this stupid justice system. That's why when I found out I wanted to do it myself!"

"Do what?"

Shit.

"Do what, Martin? What were you going to do?"

He sighed. He was in enough trouble as it was, and besides, hopefully she might see his side of things. Putting a stop to this once and for all.

"I had a suspicion she might have been allowed back home. I spoke to a friend at the facility where Claire was housed and I was told that was where she was, so I went there to check for myself. They were right. I saw her walking around the lake, looking like she didn't have a care in the world. It's not fucking fair, Kathy! The system that pays my wages is screwed! She should never have been allowed to return.

"I sat in my car watching her chat and laugh with the fishermen, and I thought about our daughter being chopped into little pieces like she was some kind of fucking animal, and I decided there and then. If the justice system won't make her pay, I will. I went to her house the other night when you were asleep, fully prepared to kill her myself. But she wasn't there. Turns out she was here instead. I probably missed her by minutes."

Kathleen looked shocked. This was totally against the character who fervently believed in the justice system and that no one should take matters into the own hands or anarchy would ensue. So in that sense he understood her reaction, but then, that was before his family had been thrust into their own horror story.

"You were gonna kill her?" she asked softly. "And what if you'd got caught? What if she killed you instead? You were willing to risk leaving us without a husband and father? How selfish can you be?! You should have phoned the authorities, lie if necessary. And now, because of that, we're without not one but both of our children! Fuck! If only she hadn't seen me the ot—"

Her jaws snapped shut, eyes widening.

Now it was Martin's turn for his eyes to widen, glare at her in disbelief.

"So yeah, this is your fault. You should ha—"

"What did you just say? You knew, too, didn't you? I knew it, the way you've been acting lately. Not wanting to talk about her. Acting as though everything was fine again. Let me guess, you went to her house to check, same as I did?"

Kathleen sighed, just as Martin had done. "Yes, I did. I had to know. I knew she wasn't in Wales. The way you spoke to Michael, I could see you were lying. You're not very good at it, so yes, I did go. And same as you I saw her there, looking happy as could be. So yeah, fuck it. I went into Bradwell to fill a petrol cannister up and burn that bitch's house down, but she saw me. She was standing outside the petrol station.

"She fucking laughed at me, Martin! She fucking laughed! Asked me how Tania was!"

Kathleen burst out crying and buried her head in Martin's chest. Things were going from disastrous to outright unbelievable. She'd actually bumped into

Claire? Was asked how Tania was? Martin was finding it difficult to breathe. His chest was tight, heart feeling like it had grown to twice its size, impeding the oxygen reach his lungs. How could things have gotten to this? It should have stopped with Tania's death, then maybe the healing process would have allowed them to start over again given time. Maybe even have another baby. And yet, it was as if they were being made to pay over and over again for someone else's crime. They didn't deserve any of this, and neither did Michael or Tania.

"Let's do it," he muttered.

Kathleen lifted her head and looked at him.

"Let's fucking do it together. Now. Before the detectives bring her in for questioning. Even if they prove she violated her parole, she might get ten years. She'll be out again before she's even thirty. You wanna hang around for her second release? Because I don't."

Kathleen said nothing, appeared to be considering the possibilities. Then, she gripped his hand in hers and whispered in his ear.

"Yes!"

Chapter 32

Claire knew exactly what was going on, because after leaving Michael's presents, she had gone and hid behind a tree to watch things unfold. It had been a long night but very much worth it. For a while, she had debated with herself as to whether Martin would phone the police or prefer his own personal agenda. When the police did arrive, she had been mildly surprised; perhaps he'd had second thoughts and had chickened out. When she was about to go home, someone else knocked on the door. It was an elderly-looking person who looked nothing like a detective, so she had creeped up the garden path, lifted the letterbox, and eavesdropped on the conversation. This had been interesting too. She guessed Michael might be a little upset and shocked, but taking him to Northgate was a bonus. Almost anyway, because she would much prefer to have killed him herself. Once agreed upon, Claire quickly ran and hid again and watched Michael being taken to the car. They practically had to carry him, the kid shuffling and dragging his feet, head and body swaying back and forth. Had they let go of him he would surely have fallen to the ground. This kid wasn't going to be any good to anyone from now on.

She returned home and waited for the inevitable knock on the door, staying up almost all night. But it never came, which she found surprising. Had they told the police about Claire or pretended they knew nothing? She had an idea it was the latter and soon, one or both of them would be coming for her. Which was just fine, but first, other matters needed attending to.

She woke up the next morning, and after feeding both the human pig and the ones outside, then collecting from the fishermen, she headed to the bus stop. Just as it arrived and she hopped on, she noticed a young woman leaning against a tree across the narrow road. Claire guessed her to be around the same age as she was, although she also thought the girl was wearing a wig for some reason as her long black hair looked unnatural. She also appeared to carry several ugly scars on her face. This wasn't the first time she'd seen her.

Claire had spotted her wandering near the farm several times over the last couple weeks, never actually coming inside the place but Claire was well aware of her presence. At first, she thought it was a detective keeping an eye on her, then maybe a neighbour or someone that recognised her. She'd considered creeping up on her and scaring her or asking her what the fuck she wanted, but there was something about her that wasn't quite right; she wasn't exactly hiding, but at the same time she wasn't making herself visible to everyone. She was always near something she could hide behind if necessary. And now that she had gotten a better look at her, she knew for sure it was no detective—she was too young, for one thing—so she could only be someone who knew about Claire. A reporter maybe, who had cancer or some illness, hence the wig, or someone who had got into a nasty fight with someone.

For a moment she was tempted to tell the driver to stop so she could confront her, but she didn't have time right now. She would have to wait and trust her better judgement; there were more important things to attend to.

She did her shopping and soon returned home, stopping by the pig pens, something she'd been doing on a regular basis to collect what she needed. She also took and killed another of the piglets recently born. It was time to make lunch for Daddy. His last.

As always, her father was slumped on the sofa half asleep, an almost empty bottle of whiskey beside him. The man looked dead or like he might die at any moment. The doctor came once a week to check up on him, scold him for continuing to smoke and drink, but it had no effect on him. Privately the doctor told Claire he was worried the man wouldn't see it to the following year unless he took more care of himself. Claire feigned worry and concern and told him she'd start hiding the alcohol and tobacco. She also said she was doing her best to make sure he at least ate healthily. "Bloody well rich in protein and vitamins," were her words. The doctor thanked her and reminded her to make sure he also took his medication, something she most certainly had been doing the last two weeks.

"Hey, Dad. Time for your injection again before lunch. I'm gonna make something real special for you today."

She sat beside him with the syringe in her hand. He squirmed as though afraid of her presence, which he was. Ever since she brought Gary home and fucked and killed him, Kenny had tried to keep out of her way. Whenever their eyes met at the dinner table, he was quick to avert her gaze and start playing with his food. If she tried to make conversation—just because she liked to see him uncomfortable and suffering—he barely responded with a nod of the head or a grunt. Kenny was doing everything he could to keep out of her way, like he was hoping she might suddenly forget he even existed. But that wasn't going to happen. It even excited her sexually to see the pathetic man acting so terrified around her. And it was for a good reason.

Kenny tried to resist, but he was in no shape or condition to do so. The doctor said his heart was in bad shape and a heart attack was possible, even probable unless he gave up the booze and tobacco. Claire had an idea the man wanted to die anyway; he deserved to, but it was going to be on her terms, not God's.

"C'mon, Dad, you know you have to take your medication. Not gonna be bad, are you? Not gonna be naughty, are you? Remember when I was a little girl and was naughty? You used to punish me, didn't you. Don't want me to punish you, do you?"

He shook his head.

"Good. Can you remember the things you used to do to me? When you used to come into my room and night and make me do things? Can you, Dad?"

"I...I'm sorry. I didn't mean to. I was sick."

"Yes, you were sick. You still are. But I'm gonna make sure you get better. You know, I can still taste it even now. At the back of my throat. I used to wake up screaming, thinking there was a monster in the room that was gonna eat me. And in a way, I was right, wasn't I? There was a monster, but instead of eating me, I was kinda, like, eating it, wasn't I?"

He looked away, ashamed and embarrassed. She could have stabbed him through the heart right there and then.

"You fucking look at me when I'm talking to you." She gripped his face and turned it towards her.

"I had to look at you when you stuck your fucking cock in my mouth, you look at me now."

She injected the syringe into his arm. The same liquid she'd been injecting every day for over a week. Claire emptied the pig's blood into his vein and pulled out the syringe. "There, see, that better? Once a pig, always a pig. Can you squeal for me, Daddy? Can you squeal like the pig you are? Or would you like me to squeal instead? Like I did when I begged you not to put it in my mouth anymore?"

Tears falling from bloodshot eyes, Kenny refused the luxury of looking away. She held the syringe so it was pointed at his eyeball. "You wanna know what it was like? What it felt like to have something alien and unnatural put inside you? Do you, Daddy? You wanna know?"

"Please, Claire, I'm sorry. I know I deserve everything and more, but I'm sick and ill now. I'll be dead soon, anyway, and you can live your life. Just…just don't hurt me. Please."

"Why shouldn't I? Look what you caused. What you made. You, Mum, everyone. Even that fucking little brat whose body I cut up and left for them to find. You did that. You and Mum. If she was here now, I'd do the same to her. So come on, Daddy, let's do it again. Just like before. Get your cock out."

Kenny's eyes widened and his jaw dropped. She didn't know what he had been expecting her to say or do, but it certainly wasn't that. He tried to squirm away from her. She gripped his face tighter and, with her other hand, pulled his filthy cock out. It sat there wrinkled and sweating. It was obvious he hadn't showered in days because the pungent odour of stale sweat rose to greet her.

"What's wrong, Daddy? You're not all hard now like you used to be when you showed it to me. Not impotent in your old age, are you? That would be a shame. Shall I suck it for you, Daddy, like in the good old days?" she asked as she gripped it between her fingers and slowly began to massage it.

He grimaced, tears falling freely. "Please stop. I was sick, I told you. I needed help. I couldn't help myself."

"Your own fucking daughter. I was a baby, for God's sake! A fucking baby. You was doing it from the moment I was born, wasn't you?"

He nodded weakly.

"Say it!"

"Yes, I was!" he bawled.

"So why don't you want to now? Or am I too old for you now?"

"Just kill me! Get it over with. I deserve it."

"Yes, you do. But you're not getting away with it that easy."

She pulled out a roll of duct tape and a knife from a small purse. "I guess you more than anyone know that pigs will eat anything, right? Even their own shit, the water they shit in. I've seen them do it. You're a pig too. Literally. I've been injecting you with their blood ever since I returned. And now, you're gonna show me how much of a pig you really are."

Claire stretched his flaccid cock and cut it off at the base in one neat slice. Kenny screamed and tried to clutch at the wound to prevent the blood from escaping, but she pushed him back. The blood drained from his face instantly. But before he could pass out from blood loss, she quickly covered the injury with a strip of duct tape.

"Now, you sit still, don't move or you'll hurt yourself. I'm going to make lunch, be back in a minute."

He'd be too weak to move, and she'd taken his mobile phone, so she was totally confident he wouldn't be going anywhere or calling for help. She was whistling as she chopped up the dead pig, removing the bones, flies already settling on it. When it was cut up into small, manageable pieces, she poured some of it into an electric blender until it was a mushy, red goo. Then she threw in her father's penis and did the same. Once she was satisfied, she returned to her father, who was deathly white, groaning, and had almost fallen to the floor. She helped him sit up again and handed him the large, plastic cup.

"Medicine time, Daddy. Drink up."

Claire squeezed his cheeks, forcing his mouth open, and slowly poured the concoction down his throat. He spluttered, showering them both in crimson gore that ran down his chin and chest. She clapped a hand over his mouth and kept it there until he swallowed it. She repeated until the cup was empty.

"There, better? Taste good?"

He tried to throw it all up, so she put her hand over his mouth again until it passed. Once she was confident it had, she helped him to his feet.

"Come on, time for a walk."

Feebly resisting, she dragged him outside to the

pig pens, directly to the male, the most aggressive of them all. She had an idea and took him to a recently emptied one, still full of pig shit and hay.

"In you go. I want to see you act like the pig you are."

She pushed him inside, and he collapsed onto the hard, wet ground. He didn't look to have much life left in him, so she was going to have to be quick.

"You have two choices, Daddy. I can let you die slowly and very painfully or nice and fast. What do you prefer?"

"Please, get help. Call an ambulance," he begged, blood and bits of pig stuck to his lips and face.

"Nope. Not gonna happen. I'll ask once more: fast or slow?"

He was sobbing now, clawing at the hay, trying to drag himself out. "Fast!" he finally managed.

"Good. Okay, so first, I want you to eat the pig shit in the water trough. Nice and soft for you. Do it. And I want you to grunt as you do so."

Kenny tried to babble for help, to be put out of his misery once and for all, but she refused. "If you don't do as you're told, I'll feed you to the pigs. And you know I will."

Struggling to keep his balance, Kenny crawled over to the dead fly and urine-infested trough and began to pick at the mouldy old pig shit floating in there. Every time he raised his head to gag and vomit, she pushed his head into the trough. When he did throw up, it floated to the surface, and she made him eat that too. After about ten minutes, and when there was nothing left to throw up, he finished eating the soggy mess. His body and face was covered in a combination of blood, piss, and shit.

"See, Daddy, wasn't so hard, was it! You really are a pig now! You dirty, filthy, disgusting piece of shit."

She dragged the sobbing man to his feet and dragged him to the pen with the boar inside. As she unlocked the gate, she whispered in his ear, "I lied about not feeding you to the pig. I hope it eats you from the feet up so you get to watch. I want to watch you suffer and squeal and grunt. I fucking hate you for what you made me into, and I hope to see you in hell soon."

She pushed him inside and locked the gate again. The other pen was where the sow had given birth to the male's babies. Since then, the boar had become grumpy and aggressive, trying to jump over the brick wall to get to the sow again. Upon smelling the sow's piss and shit on Kenny, it immediately began grunting and snorting when Kenny fell to the ground. Before he could even attempt to get up again, the pig was on him. Unfortunately, Claire did not get her wish.

The Jabali's strong teeth clamped around Kenny's head and squeezed. Her father's muffled screams were still audible as one of the tusks pierced his throat, coming out the other side, great jets of blood shot like fountains into the air. The pig's head thrashed from side to side, grunting ferociously, eyes bloodshot and feral. Kenny was thrown around like a doll. One particularly violent thrust saw half of Kenny's face torn off, revealing the skull and glistening muscle tissue beneath. It swallowed the flesh and resumed with its apparent desire to rip the man's head off. It didn't take long. There was a loud crack as his spine snapped and the head came loose.

It reminded Claire of seeing a dog carrying its favourite ball around at the park.

The Jabali spat out the head and began slathering and tearing at the rest of the precious meat. With that, Claire decided she'd seen enough. She was only slightly surprised to discover it hadn't excited her sexually at all, only stirred a mild satisfaction that one more monster in the world was finally gone. Claire headed back to the house with not even a smile on her face.

That changed an hour later when there was a loud knock on the door.

Chapter 33

When Claire went to answer the door, she was smirking. It seemed the woman who had been stalking her had finally found the courage to ask for an interview, no doubt for quite a lucrative sum. There would be promises of hiding her identity and location in exchange for her story. She would ask what was going on in her mind when she killed Tania. It would make for quite a story too. Her mother's abuse and complete lack of affection, her father who showed his affection in other ways. But Claire had no need or intention of answering questions or sparking the nation's fury once more. The last thing she wanted was to bring attention to herself. But when she opened the door, ready to politely tell the woman she wasn't interested, and saw the Forsyths standing there instead, she was only mildly surprised. Mildly, because she also guessed this would happen.

"Oh, hi there. What a surprise. I didn't expect to see you two again. I'd invite you in for a coffee, but I've ran out. How's it going?"

Both wore solemn expressions, yet hate burned in their eyes. They looked like they wanted to kill her right there. Claire had seen Kathleen up close and thought she looked as though twenty years older, but Martin strangely hadn't changed too much, with barely a wrinkle on his face as though he was above grief and everything that came with it.

"We just wanted to speak with you. We have questions," said Kathleen. "Answer them for us and we promise you'll never see us again. Now that

Michael is in hospital we're selling the house and moving, starting over, but we need to know. Can we come in?"

"Well, my dad's asleep right now. Sleeps like a pig most times but also awakens easily. I wouldn't want to disturb the poor man."

"We'll be quick and won't make any noise, I promise."

Claire stepped aside and led them to the kitchen, inviting them to sit at the table.

"Excuse the mess. We just finished eating."

The counter was still covered in bits of dried intestines and organs and blood from chopping up the pig. The food blender was a bright red colour, sticky lumps glued to its sides. Upon seeing it, Kathleen looked like she might throw up any second – a nasty reminder of another time. Which was precisely why Claire had brought them here and not to the living room.

"So, what can I do for you? Sorry to hear about Michael, by the way. I liked him, nice kid."

As she taunted them with her words, acting as though meeting old friends for the first time in years, Martin had to keep looking away, fiddling with the buttons on his shirt. But Kathleen was the complete opposite. Not once did she take her eyes off Claire. She was grinding her teeth or biting her tongue or something, lower jaw moving side to side. This was the one Claire would have to be careful with, her maternal instincts in overdrive. Most mothers would do anything to protect their children, give their own life if necessary, and here was a woman sitting face to face with her daughter's killer. In a way, Claire was jealous. They represented everything she had been denied as a child.

"I want to know why," said Kathleen. "Why kill my baby? She did nothing to you. Neither did any of us. Okay, we could have made more effort, call child services, the police, whoever, but we had our own lives to live. You could have told us what you were going through. We had no idea. But that doesn't excuse what you did. How you did it. Why?"

"Well, I guess it seemed right at the time. All I wanted was a little attention and love, and when I thought I was getting it, you had your little baby. You swapped me for it and kicked me out. I was angry, I suppose, so decided I should slaughter and gut her, like our pigs. All humans are pigs, really, not a lot of difference, and that was no exception. I wanted to take her home, cut up her body, and make a stew for my parents. But I guess I changed my mind."

She shrugged, raised her hands. *Whadaya do? Life's a bitch, right?*

A solitary tear trickled down Kathleen's face. Martin said nothing but looked like he might faint.

"And that justifies what you did? Doing…that to my baby girl? It doesn't make any sense. She was totally *innocent!* We didn't ask you to come into our lives. We would have continued letting you come over. We did *nothing* to make you do that."

"Story of my life. That's what they all say. '*Wasn't my fault.*' Isn't it funny how we all blame everyone else for our shortcomings, our failures? Your husband and son said I smelled like a pig one time. I heard them laughing at me when they thought I wasn't there. So, who's the pig now? If I hadn't fucked up, I was going to kill you all too. Starting with Michael. I was going to cut his tongue out and make him eat it while he squealed. I might still do so, actually."

"You're sick. A sick, fucked up, evil monster," said Martin finally. "Prison is too good for the likes of you. Not even Northgate. Everyone else was right, after all. I was wrong. The justice system doesn't work. It doesn't punish monsters for their crimes. Not legally or morally. Monsters like you deserve the full punishment."

"And is that what you've both come to do? Make me pay for what I did? Well, go ahead, fuck do I care."

It was said as a bluff because she didn't really think either had it in them to carry out the threat. Maybe Kathleen, but it was one thing to be overcome with rage and grief and make threats, but to kill another human being was beyond most. Besides, Claire had a knife in her pocket, and she had no problems whatsoever killing another.

"Don't you even regret what you did to an innocent baby girl? You have absolutely no remorse at all?"

"Remorse or regret isn't gonna bring your fucking girl back, is it, so what's the point? Oh, I'm so sorry. It was an accident. I didn't mean to, please forgive me. I'll buy you another. Right," she said in a mock voice. "And anyway, no, I don't. You two feel any remorse for pushing me away? You must have seen the bruises, the cigarette burns on my arms. The shabby, unwashed clothes. And you pretended not to, so fuck you both. The only regret I have is not eating your little Tania. Her little heart would have been so tasty."

It happened so fast that even though Claire was expecting it, she still didn't react in time. All the while she had been waiting for Kathleen to launch herself at her, Martin sobbing like a baby, but it was the other way around. While Kathleen glared at Claire in horror, Martin suddenly jumped up and bundled her to the floor, a punch to the face leaving her stunned. Before she could grab the knife in her back pocket and slit his throat, Martin had her in a headlock, pushing her onto her back, while his other hand twisted her arm up high.

"You fucking, monstrous, evil bitch. You ruined all our lives, killed our baby just because you felt left out. Well, don't worry, because where you're going it's full of evil fuckers just like you. And I'm not talking Northgate. Kathy, get the rope."

Kathleen quickly hurried outside and came back with a length of rope they must have hidden by the front door. There was no point in Claire even trying to struggle—Martin must be double her weight, at least a foot taller, and the grip he had on her was solid. But at the same time, if she had to die, so be it. She didn't fear death, only a life of solitude, which to her was far scarier. And now that her dad was dead, she didn't think it would be long before someone came to check on him. His doctor, for example. Her life had been pretty much over before it had even started. The future looked no brighter.

Claire made no attempt to resist as her hands were tied behind her back.

"If she tries anything, kick her, stab her, whatever, but don't kill her," said Martin, panting. "I'm gonna check to see if her dad's asleep in the living room. He's just as guilty as she is. This whole fucking family is."

He left and returned a few moments later after having checked upstairs too.

"He's not here. She was lying. Where is he?" he demanded.

"Well, I'm not entirely sure. He might be sitting in my pig's stomach, or he might be one big lump of shit already splattered on the pen floor. Who cares?"

"Not me, for sure. Oh well, one less to worry about. Even better. Kathy, go get the other thing we brought, would you?"

She hesitated for a moment, as if unsure. Claire caught it immediately, making her wonder what they had planned for her. Perhaps they were going to do the same to her as she had done to Tania. An eye for an eye, which should have gone against all Martin's beliefs. But then, she reasoned, a major tragedy could do that to a person.

"Kathy, you hear me? Go get the other thing."

She snapped out of her daze and left.

"Feeling better now, Mr Forsyth? A chance to dish out a little vengeance. How does it feel?"

"I don't feel anything. Just doing what should have been done years ago. It's not fair, and it's not right. I can't let you continue haunting my family and let you get away with it. I know now. The criminal system is wrong. They should never have banished the death penalty. It was there for a reason. People like you don't deserve to live, so if the law won't stop you, I will. Once we've finished with you, I'll resign and do something else. There's no point trying to understand the minds of monsters like you because you don't even understand yourselves. How could we ever hope to cure and prevent such despicable acts from happening? It's impossible. You're nothing more than mindless evil dressed in human skin. There is no cure."

In that, Claire had to agree. She would never have stopped killing unless she was dead or in prison. It was built into her now, a killing machine without heart or soul, something spawned in some foul wasteland that had drained her of all empathy and love for anything and anyone. Perhaps it was best she died now so she could try and find peace and comfort elsewhere.

Kathleen returned with a petrol cannister, and Claire knew her fate. If she hadn't bumped into Kathleen that day, she'd probably be dead already. Martin dragged her into the living room and threw her on the sofa, then took the cannister from his wife. Kathleen looked on, but once again Claire caught that look of doubt in her eyes. It was the moment of truth, and it seemed that despite all the hate she had for Claire, doubts were creeping in. Claire had evidently got it wrong when it came to who hurt the most. Martin poured the liquid over Claire and the sofa.

"You wanna do it, Kathy? Put an end to this once and for all?"

But Kathy was standing there, not apparently listening. She couldn't take her eyes of Claire, glaring down at her as though staring at some disgusting creature.

"Kathy, you okay? No backing out now, you know. It was your idea. Think of our baby and what she did. What she did to Michael. She deserves this."

At that, she turned to face her husband as though woken from a trance. But she still looked far from convinced. Tears streamed down her face, her hands shaking. Maybe Claire wasn't going to die, after all. But if Kathleen did convince Martin to let her go, she wasn't going to prison, of that she had no doubt. These two would be dead before they even finished dialling the police.

"I…I don't know, Martin. She deserves it, yes, but this isn't right. If we kill her, we're just as bad as she is. You told me that yourself years ago. Killing her is the easy way out. She should spend the rest of her life in prison, suffering every single day."

"Kathy, we already spoke about this. What if she doesn't go to prison? And even if she does, she could be out in five to seven years. You wanna go through it all again? We need to put a stop to this right now. Terminate it. Here, do it." He handed her a lighter.

But just then, when it seemed Martin had convinced her, there was movement in the hallway. All turned their heads to see who it was. And when the person stepped into the living room, it was Martin who reacted first.

"Sarah? Is that you?"

It was the woman that had been following Claire the last few days. As she stepped into the light, her injuries were even clearer to see. She had multiple scars on her arms, face, and neck. There was a skin graft on her arm. Her nose had obviously been broken, as well, and she walked as though in pain, hobbling slightly. But Claire still had no idea who she was and whether she was here to help her or aid in her demise.

"Yes, it is me. I'd been watching this woman for a while then saw you two turn up. Looks like you beat me to it. I was thinking of doing something similar."

Martin seemed to be in utter shock for reasons Claire didn't know.

"I've seen you following and watching me. Who are you? Come to release me or help these fine people do what they came for?"

"You know, I was in a similar position to you. Not once, but twice. I managed to escape, but I don't think you'll be so lucky. I just needed to confirm you were who I thought you were, and I was going to kill you myself. They beat me to it. I don't know if I should be glad or not."

"If you were in a similar position to me, you're not being very helpful about it. Shouldn't you be trying to set me free or something? Besides, what have I ever done to you?"

"You misunderstand. And now that I'm here, I think I'll stay around and watch the fun."

"Sarah, you...you shouldn't really be here, you know. I'm glad to see you're okay at least, but if the police happened to come, you're a wanted person," said Martin.

"It's okay. I don't mind. Carry on."

Martin turned to Kathleen, still holding the lighter and listening to the conversation. "Kathy?"

"Okay, but turn her over first. I don't want to see her...her face when it goes up."

Martin pushed her onto her stomach and quickly jumped back so the fumes wouldn't set him on fire too. Kathleen ignited the Zippo and edged closer. Claire closed her eyes and waited.

Chapter 34

"Stop."

Martin and Kathleen halted, while Claire rolled back onto her stomach to face Sarah. She held a knife to Kathleen's throat and had every intention of using it if necessary. Carefully, she took the Zippo from Kathleen's hand and put it in her pocket. With the amount of fumes in the room, chances are they would all have exploded into balls of fire. But this wasn't the main reason for stopping proceedings.

"Sarah, what are you doing?" asked Martin.

"Untie her."

"Sarah, wait. I don't know what the matter is, but she deserves to die for what she did. She brutally murdered and butchered our tiny baby. Many years ago. She's been taunting us about it. She broke into our home and left a dead, cut up pig under Michael's pillow. She said herself she was going to kill us too. Just like Andrew and those other savages that tortured you, Sarah. She is just as bad."

Sarah knew perfectly well the details surrounding what Claire had done. She had read about the case on the internet not long after deciding to seek anonymity, tired of therapists and psychologists and being harassed day and night to do interviews. She never wanted to forget her past, but she certainly wanted others to do so. Sarah had first decided on what her future might hold just after killing Andrew and his friends and reflected more on it while recovering from her injuries. For two weeks she lay in hospital, answering police questions while journalists pretending to be doctors sneaked into her room with hidden mobile phones in their pockets to record her words. Therapists and psychologists—Martin included—wanted to probe her mind as though she was a new species of animal. She became sick of it all. Not once did they want to know how she had survived for so long, how she felt about it. All they cared about was the grizzly details surrounding what they did to her and how she avenged her kidnappers. There was even talk on TV that she deserved to go to prison, that she was a monster and had no right carrying out justice by herself. There was a criminal system set in place for that.

And so, once she received her father's life insurance money, she fled and rented a small flat in nearby Gorleston. Most of her hair had been missing anyway, but even so, she bought a wig and tried to keep hidden from the public while seeking out others like Andrew. No one, she decided, should have to go through what she did. She would make the kidnappers and torturers pay instead of hoping a crooked legal system would bring justice. It was then she stumbled upon Claire and what she had done to Tania, while coincidentally a serial killer was targeting men in the area. Even more coincidental was that it had been Martin's baby, the man who insisted in being the one to interview Sarah during her rehabilitation. A little more research and the woman at the farm that bore a striking resemblance to young Claire answered her question. But it was while watching the grounds and seeing Martin then his wife doing the same thing, she immediately guessed what was going on. And from the look of things right now, she had been right. But it was all wrong.

"Perhaps she does deserve to pay for what she did, but you're forgetting something. She's not real. She's not herself. If anyone deserves to die, it's her parents, and they're already dead. Let her go."

Martin and Kathleen looked stunned. It took several seconds for either to say anything, Kathleen being the first.

"Look, Sarah. I know what you went through, and it was terrible and should never have happened, but this woman is exactly the same as those kids who put you through all that. She's a callous, remorseless killer who won't stop until we're dead too. Our son is now in a mental hospital because of her. We had to admit him tonight before coming here. No one is safe from her until she's dead. And that's what we're going to do."

All the time Claire was laying there, listening to the conversation with equal amounts of surprise and delight on her face. Whether Claire knew about Sarah's experiences she didn't know, but this woman had been abused and worse from her parents, turned into a monster and could not be held responsible for how she had turned out. That she very probably would go on to kill these two as well was highly probable, but Sarah wasn't willing to see a victim just like her suffer this way.

"Untie her, Kathleen. I totally agree, but this isn't the way. Phone the police if you like and see what happens. After that, it's on you. But I can't stand here and watch you set fire to another victim like myself."

Reluctantly, Kathleen did as she was told, now in tears, mumbling about justice. Claire sat up and rubbed her wrists.

"Well, that was very generous of you. A victim you say? Maybe we should team up."

"Don't get clever. What you did was still despicable, but I understand it. You lost any sense of empathy or right or wrong. A child abused by everyone one way or the other. I'm going to leave right now. I'll leave you to it."

And with that, Sarah let Kathleen go and quickly hurried off into the night. Only recently she had seen on the news about a terrible incident nearby. A young girl by the name of Angela had gone missing, among others. It was suspected she had been taken to be used by a child sex-trafficking gang, terrible videos of young kids being violently raped and tortured then the videos sold on the dark web. This was something that held Sarah's attention. It seemed her work was never-ending.

Chapter 35

Claire had been expecting a lot of things to happen, but not that. First, she had waited for an agonising death, then for this Sarah to start taking loads of photos or something as a reporter, and then after hearing who Sarah was, for imminent death once more. What she most certainly hadn't expected was to be set free and left to carry on where she left off if she so desired. Martin and Kathleen evidently hadn't expected this new turn of events, either, because now all three of them were together in the room, none saying anything, looking at each other back and forth. The first thing Martin did was instantly go to his wife and embrace her protectively.

"Well, that was fun, wasn't it?" she said. "She some kind of avenger or something, like a superhero? She looks like she got into a fight with someone, anyway. And came off worse."

"You have no idea," said Martin. "Some things she said were true, others not. She went through a lot, more than you ever did, and her brain is muddled. What she did was in self-defence, unlike you. You're just evil, plain and simple."

"That so? Well, it kinda leaves us in an awkward situation, doesn't it. You wanna carry on where you left off or you gonna get the fuck out of my house? I'll call the police and have you arrested for breaking and entering. Poor, defenceless woman like me scared to death. And while you're in prison, I'll visit Michael for you. Tell him everything's fine. I'll visit him a lot."

Such was his hatred and the rage surely bubbling

away in his veins, Martin was foaming at the mouth, as though rabid. But just as Claire stood up, preparing herself for the inevitable confrontation, he punched her in the face so hard and fast she barely saw it. One minute she was standing up, the next she was sprawled on the floor.

"Kathy, quick, find another lighter. I don't care what Sarah said, this ends here and now. Go!"

Given everything that had just occurred, Claire had almost forgotten she'd had petrol poured over her despite the potent smell of it. It didn't matter now, though, because she thought her nose was broken and she couldn't smell anything. She felt the warm blood gushing down her chin, some entering her mouth, and she swallowed it. It tasted good, reviving old memories, and a surge of adrenaline gave her the strength necessary to push herself up.

"Mmm," she said. "My blood tastes just like Tania's did. I wonder if yours tastes the same. Shall we find out?"

"You fucking bitch. Why won't you just die? Kathy! Hurry up! I wanna watch this bitch burn."

Kathleen yelled something from somewhere in the house. Martin drew his arm back to punch her again, eyes blazing with determination and hate. But he made a crucial mistake. They all had.

In full view of everyone, yet completely ignored by all except Claire, was her father's half empty whiskey bottle on the coffee table. Just as Martin swung again, she ducked, grabbed the bottle, and smashed it over the top of his head as hard as she could. He crumpled instantly. Claire wasted no time. She might have accepted imminent death ten minutes ago, but not anymore. As Martin groaned and tried to push himself to his feet, she stepped back and kicked him in the kidneys. Kathleen could return at any second with a lighter and stop her, so she had to be fast. The bottle having broken when connecting with his skull, she squatted and thrust the sharp, broken blades into his face with both hands, turning it left and right as she did so for maximum effect. Part of it went into his right eyeball, sinking in with ease, causing a small jet of some colourless secretion to shoot into the air. Martin tried to scream, but the other end of the bottle had sliced open his lips, and was now sawing through his teeth. He tried to roll over, clutch at the bottle, but Claire was firmly kneeling on him, revelling in the amount of blood pouring from his mouth and down his throat. Then suddenly, she was hit over the head with some kind of blunt object, causing her to shudder and howl in pain.

"Get off him! Martin! You bastard, what are you doing?"

It was Kathleen, having returned, and evidently empty-handed or Claire would be ablaze. Without wasting time, she wrenched the bottle from Martin's face and swung blindly, hitting Kathleen across the face, which caused her to stagger backwards and trip over. Despite the immense pain and the blood loss, Martin still tried to get up, so Claire rammed the bottle once more into his face, this time piercing his other eyeball, leaving him blind. He howled, arms flailing as Claire raised the bottle and again and again rammed it into his face, then went for the neck, using the sharp edge to cut a line across his throat. It erupted, showering her in warm, fresh blood, much of it going down her throat, which she swallowed as she screamed in rage. Already tiring, she turned to see Kathleen getting up. It was now impossible to see Martin's face because it was totally covered in blood and broken shards of glass. What she thought might be a piece of his tongue was stuck to one broken shard. Bits of flesh and skin clung to others, lumps strewn around Martin's fading body like confetti.

"Martin! Stop, you're gonna kill him!" yelled Kathleen as she stumbled towards them.

The bottle now slick in Claire's hands, she took advantage of Kathleen's disorientated state and sank the bottle into her between the legs, her flimsy skirt offering no protection whatsoever. It must have found a home, because as Kathleen screamed and collapsed, Claire couldn't remove the bottle. She waited until Kathleen was on her back to yank it out. Immediately, Kathleen's legs ran red, as though suffering an impromptu period. Claire cut a deep gash across her face, slicing off her cheeks, then returned her attention to Martin. He was barely alive now, his face unrecognisable, missing great lumps of flesh, leaving gaping holes where the blood ran down into the back of his mouth. His eyeballs had been ripped out during the destruction of his face, craters filling up with crimson gore. His cheeks flapped like thick pages of a book as he rolled his head feebly from side to side, red bubbles blowing from his mouth as if he'd been eating strawberry or cherry bubble-gum. Now completely at his mercy, the threat gone, she could recover her strength and admire her work. With Kathleen barely conscious, they were both her playthings.

Leaving them both semi-conscious, Claire headed into the kitchen to get something to drink and quench her growing thirst. She saw her knife on the floor she'd intended on using on them previously. When she picked it up and rose, she happened to catch a glance of herself in a small mirror hanging on the wall. She looked as though she'd just taken a blood bath, her face splattered in Martin's gore. She smiled and licked her lips.

"Who's a piggie too, huh?" she muttered and returned to the living room.

Kathleen was waking, reaching out for her husband with shaking arms before they flopped back to the floor again. Claire squatted beside her.

"Hey, Kathy, how you feeling? Need anything?"

Kathleen swiped at her as though swatting away a fly.

"Well, not to worry. You'll be with darling Tania soon. I heard they put her back together again with staples. Is that true?"

Kathleen tried to respond by hitting her but missed. With so much blood loss, Claire guessed her world right now was blurry and fading fast.

"You could have prevented all this all those years ago, but you chose not to. I'm not at fault for who I am. Your friend, Sarah, said the same thing. Bye, Kathy."

She cut open Kathleen's skirt and knickers then rolled her onto her stomach. A vicious gash just above her vagina showed where the bottle had entered. Claire took the knife and slowly pushed it up Kathleen's vagina as far as it would go, turning the blade three hundred and sixty degrees with both hands, gripped the knife, and tore upwards as she pulled it out. Now, instead of two holes there, it was a large, fleshy one, anus and vagina united as a whole. Claire returned to the kitchen, collected the remains of the slaughtered piglet, then came back and shoved them all into the bleeding hole, leaving the piglet's head sticking out as though she was giving birth to it.

"There, see! You're a piggie too! Ain't that cute!"

Now that she'd overcome the exertion of what she'd done to Martin, other sensations returned to her. The sensations were so potent and overwhelming she thought she might drown in them just as the Forsyths were drowning in their own blood. She looked around, at herself, seeing red everywhere, and once again she was transported to when she was a sad, young girl staring into the empty cavity of the slaughtered pig, wanting to crawl inside it and hide. She was standing in the Forsyth's kitchen staring in awe at her masterpiece while Tania's dead face looked back up at her, expressionless. She saw the old woman swirling the pig's blood around in the bucket, some of it splashing onto her face. Claire was all those things and more now, a pig herself, but slaughtered not in body but in mind and spirit. Her soul was as empty as that pig's stomach had been. She was Tania, broken, literally into countless parts, never to be reconstructed again, a puzzle forever uncompleted. The memories and images of her life were so intense she sobbed, and it was only when she looked down at herself and saw that her hand was furiously rubbing her clitoris she also understood she had become as the two she despised most of all in her young life.

Her parents.

Because she wasn't sobbing in pity, it was for the ecstasy of her actions. And she needed more.

She rushed upstairs, collected her mother's old dildo, and in the middle of the soaking wet carpet downstairs, thrust the sex toy in and out of her body as though her life depended upon it, grunting and squealing like a pig, wanting it harder, deeper, until she thought it might tear the walls of her own vagina just as Kathleen's were. And when she came, she screamed. She screamed in ecstasy, in rage, in helplessness, for herself and what she had become, and when she finally quietened down, she took out the dildo, crawled over to Martin, and shoved it as far down his throat as she could, just as her father had done to her on so many occasions. Only when the ripples of her lust died down did she finish off what she had set out to do to both Kathleen and Martin.

An hour later, totally exhausted, not even caring to shower when about to head off to bed, she heard the police sirens screaming as they hurtled down the dirt track towards her house, and she sighed and went to meet them.

Chapter 36

"How did you feel when you were arrested, Claire? When you knew it was all over, no more killing?"

She looks out the window for a while, no expression on her face although I detect a sense of pity. Perhaps knowing there was a whole world out there that, despite being almost twenty now, she has never really had the chance to enjoy. And not entirely through any wrongdoing of her own. Not originally. So many things people take for granted and she has known none of it. Or maybe she's just devoid of all emotion and sense of excitement. Except when it comes to killing, of course.

"Nothing, I guess. I suppose my mission in life was to ruin those that ruined me. The only one who escaped was my mother, and I sure as hell would have loved to feed her to the pigs. Maybe I would have tracked down some of those kids from school that bullied me. Maybe I would have sliced them open and forced them to eat themselves. Just to see the looks on their faces. They shouldn't have been allowed to lead normal, happy lives after what they did to me. Don't you think?"

"Children can be very cruel, Claire. Much more so than their parents. They don't really know the harm they cause, not the long-lasting effects anyway. The difference is when you killed Tania, you knew exactly what you were doing and what the results of doing it would be. Through no fault of your own, something was born inside you, full of rage. Hate. I don't think you would have ever stopped until you were caught, would you?"

"Probably not. Dunno. I don't think I could ever have maintained a proper relationship with anyone. At the slightest sense of betrayal or hurt, I would probably have killed them beforehand, so maybe it's for the best. Better for everyone."

"And you don't feel sorry in any way for Martin, Kathleen, and their son, Michael? He committed suicide, you know, shortly after hearing of his parents' death."

Absolutely no sign of surprise or regret on her face after hearing that. To her he was nothing, just another that conspired to ruin her life.

"I already told you, they deserved it. If they hadn't kicked me out, I might still be living with them now. Who knows? Sarah was a strange one, though. I'd like to see her again. I'm sure she has some fascinating stories to tell. I guess we're both pretty similar. Both went through shit but came out better for it."

"You think you came out better? You'll spend the rest of your life in prison, never to be freed again."

"I've been in prison since the moment I was born. Living in a pigsty just like my father's pigs. My mother probably gave fucking birth to me in one. None of this was my fault. I didn't ask to be born to those parents. What happened was meant to be. No regrets."

"Interesting. Tell me, Claire: would you call yourself a monster?"

"I dunno. We're all monsters. You tell me."

The end

Author's Note

Well, here we are again. The end of another Monsters book. I hope you enjoyed it. As long as people enjoy them (if enjoy is the right word), I'll keep writing them. Book 4 is already under way and this one is nasty. If you've heard of Hurtcore, you'll know what I mean…

This one was written using two true stories as the basis, involving horrific crimes with kids. The first one, and you may have heard of this case, is that of Beth Thomas. At 6 years old she stated in an extraordinary interview that she wanted to kill her brothers and parents. Beth also tortured the dog and birds. She smashed her younger brother's head repeatedly against a concrete floor, tried to push him down the stairs until there came a point she couldn't be left alone with him. She spoke like she was talking about her favourite pastime. She had no idea why she did such things or wanted to kill them, she just did. Thanks to extensive therapy, it was discovered she had RAD, Reactive Attachment Disorder, and was cured.

The second was a boy named Eric Smith, 13 years old. He had a rough upbringing, was constantly bullied and may have been sexually abused. At some point he suffered major head trauma and his personality changed. He became violent, attacking other boys at school. At 9, he was smoking a full packet of cigarettes a day, and was already having sexual urges, then around 12 he told his father and teachers he wanted to hurt someone, becoming obsessed by the fact. No one listened. So when 13, he was out stalking on his pushbike and came across a 4-year-old boy walking home alone just one block from where he lived. Eric dragged him into nearby woods and beat him to death with a large rock as well as strangling him. He flew into a rage and stomped on him. Eventually he was caught and arrested.

I wondered at first if Claire at just 8 was perhaps too young to commit her first murder—Tania—but after watching several more documentaries decided she wasn't. There was a huge case in England years ago where two 10-year-old boys murdered another young boy. For fun. Is Claire—or the others for that matter—responsible for what she did? There are arguments both for and against.

You may have noticed at the end of the book, Sarah hears of the disappearance of a young girl, Angela, suspected of being kidnapped by a sex trafficking ring. That will be the basis of the next book!

As always I'd like to thank everyone who helped this book come together. Heather Larson for her editing, Christ Aldridge for the cover, Angel Van Atta for formatting, and all my beta-readers and ARC readers. Thank you all so much!

Also by J. Boote

Man's Best Friend
Love You To Bits
Buried
They are all Monsters
Am I a Monster

Also by Justin Boote

Short Story Collections:
Love Wanes, Fear is Forever
Love Wanes, Fear is Forever: Volume 2
Love Wanes, Fear is Forever: Volume 3

Novels:

Serial
Combustion
Chasing Ghosts
Carnivore: Book 1 of The Ghosts of Northgate trilogy
The Ghosts of Northgate: Book 2 of The Ghosts of Northgate trilogy
A Mad World: Book 3 of The Ghosts of Northgate trilogy
The End of Things as He Knew Them (with Angel Van Atta)

The Undead Possession Series –
Book 1: Infestation
Book 2: Resurrection
Book 3: Corruption
Book 4: Legion
Book 5: Resurgence

From Wicked House Publishers
In Grandma's Room (a YA horror novel)

Short stories available on Godless
Badass
Grandmother Drinks Blood
If Flies Could Fart
A Question of Possession